NAGUIB MAHFOUZ
AKHENATEN
Dweller in Truth

Naguib Mahfouz was born in Cairo in 1911 and began writing when he was seventeen. A student of philosophy and an avid reader, his works range from reimaginings of ancient myths to subtle commentaries on contemporary Egyptian politics and culture. Over a career that lasted more than five decades, he wrote 33 novels, 13 short story anthologies, numerous plays, and 30 screenplays. Of his many works, most famous is *The Cairo Trilogy*, consisting of *Palace Walk* (1956), *Palace of Desire* (1957), and *Sugar Street* (1957), which focuses on a Cairo family through three generations, from 1917 until 1952. In 1988, he was awarded the Nobel Prize in Literature, the first writer in Arabic to do so. He died in August 2006.

THE FOLLOWING TITLES BY NAGUIB MAHFOUZ ARE
ALSO PUBLISHED BY ANCHOR BOOKS:

The Thief and the Dogs

The Beginning and the End

Wedding Song

The Beggar

Respected Sir

Autumn Quail

The Time and the Place and other stories

The Search

Midaq Alley

The Journey of Ibn Fattouma

Miramar

Adrift on the Nile

The Harafish

Arabian Nights and Days

Children of the Alley

Echoes of an Autobiography

The Cairo Trilogy:

Palace Walk

Palace of Desire

Sugar Street

AKHENATEN

Dweller in Truth

AKHENATEN

Dweller in Truth

NAGUIB MAHFOUZ

Translated by
Tagreid Abu-Hassabo

ANCHOR BOOKS
A DIVISION OF RANDOM HOUSE, INC.
NEW YORK

AN ANCHOR ORIGINAL, MARCH 2000

English translation copyright © 1998 by The American University
in Cairo Press

All rights reserved under International and Pan-American Copyright
Conventions. Published in the United States by Anchor Books,
a division of Random House, Inc., New York,
and simultaneously in Canada by
Random House of Canada Limited, Toronto.
Originally published in Arabic as *al-'A'ish fi-l-haqiqa.* Copyright © 1985
by Naguib Mahfouz.
This translation first published in paperback by
The American University in Cairo Press, Egypt, in 1998.

Library of Congress Cataloging-in-Publication data
Mahfuz, Najib, 1911–
['A'ish fi al-haqiqah. English]
Akhenaten, dweller in truth / Naguib Mahfouz ;
translated by Tagreid Abu-Hassabo.
p. cm.
ISBN 0-385-49909-4 (trade pbk.)
1. Akhenaton, King of Egypt—Fiction. I. Abu-Hassabo, Tagreid. II. Title.
PJ7846.A46A7613 2000
892.7'36—dc21 .   99-056659

www.anchorbooks.com

Printed in the United States of America
20 19 18 17 16 15 14 13 12

Contents

A K H E N A T E N

Dweller in Truth

———

The Beginning

———

It all began with a glance, a glance that grew into desire, as the ship pushed its way against the calm, strong current at the end of the flood season. The journey started from our city Sais, heading south toward Panopolis, where my sister had lived since her marriage. One late afternoon, our ship passed a strange city. It was bordered by the Nile to the west, and an imposing mountain to the east. Its buildings hinted of a past grandeur that had given way to a haunting evanescence. The roads were empty, the trees were leafless, the gates and windows closed like eyelids of the dead. A city devoid of life, inert, possessed by silence, shadowed by gloom and the spirit of death. I was dismayed at the sight of it, and I hurried to my father, who was seated, crowned with the dignity of old age, on a bench on the ship's deck.

"Father, what is wrong with this city?"

"Meriamun, this is the city of the heretic. The cursed and infidel city," he replied calmly.

I looked again with increasing excitement, as the memories flowed.

"Does no one live there?"

"That woman, the heretic's wife, she still lives in her palace—or her prison I should say. And there must be a few guards."

"Nefertiti," I murmured to myself, remembering, and wondering how she had endured her isolation.

Visions from my boyhood at my father's palace in Sais kept coming to me, of the elders' fervent debates about the whirlwind that had devastated Egypt and the whole empire. They called it the war of the deities. I remembered the stories about the young pharaoh who had rejected his ancestors' heritage, challenged the priests, and defied destiny. I recalled those hushed voices, the talk of a new religion, and the people's bewilderment, unable to choose between their old faith and their loyalty to the pharaoh. People argued about unusual events, the terrible defeat of the empire, then the triumphs followed by grief.

So here was the city of wonders, possessed by the spirit of death. And there was its mistress, a solitary prisoner sipping bitterness. My heart beat fast, desperate to learn the whole story.

"You will never accuse me of meekness hereafter, Father, for I am swept by a sacred desire, strong as the northern winds, a desire to know the truth and record it, as you did in the prime of your youth."

He glanced at me with weary eyes and said, "What is it that you want, Meriamun?"

"I want to learn everything about this city and its ruler. About the tragedy that ripped the country apart and laid waste the empire."

"But you heard everything in the temple," he replied.

"Father, the sage Qaqimna said, 'Pass no judgment upon a matter until you have heard all testimonies.'"

"But the truth in this case is evident. Besides, Akhenaten, the heretic, is dead."

"Most of his contemporaries are alive though," I replied with growing excitement, "and they are your peers and friends. An introduction from you, Father, would help open doors and reveal secrets to me. Then I could see the many facets of truth before it perishes like this city."

I insisted until finally he granted me his approval, possibly with concealed enthusiasm. For Father himself had a passion for knowledge and recording the truth, a fact that made our palace a gathering point for men of both worldly and religious affairs. Our palace was famous for its forums where stories were narrated and poetry recited, and for the great banquets of delicious duck and fine wines. Father was known among his friends as a man blessed with unique wisdom and abundant land.

He handed me some letters to deliver to the notable people who remembered that time: those who had participated closely, or from afar, and those who had experienced its bitterness as well as its sweetness.

"You have chosen your path, so walk it. May the gods protect you," said Father. "Your forefathers sought war, politics, or trade, but you, Meriamun, you seek the truth instead, and one's cause ranks as high as the determination vested in it. Be careful not to provoke the powerful, or gloat over the misfortune of those who have fallen into oblivion. Be like history, impartial and open to every witness. Then deliver a truth that is free of bias for those who wish to contemplate it."

I was happy to bid indolence farewell, and to set off along the path of history in search of truth, a path that has no beginning and no end, for it will always be extended by those who have a passion for eternal truth.

The High Priest of Amun

———

Thebes had returned to prosperity after its terrible desertion by the heretic. Once more it was the capital of the empire, its throne graced by the young pharaoh Tutankhamun. Men of peace and war returned to their positions, and the priests resumed their duties in the temples. Palaces were restored, gardens blossomed, and the temple of Amun regained its grandeur and stood proudly with its giant columns and flowering garden. The markets were filled with buyers, merchants, and goods, and the stream of wealth flowed continuously. The city was now a marvel of glory.

It was my first venture to Thebes. I was dazzled by its brilliant architecture and amazed by its vast population. I was overwhelmed by the sounds of the city and the sight of its roads, busy with carriages and carts. In comparison, my city Sais seemed like a small, quiet, obscure village.

I reached the temple of Amun at the appointed time.

A servant ushered me through the hall of grand columns and into a lateral corridor leading to the room where the high priest awaited me. I saw him in the center of the room, seated on a chair of ebony with armrests of pure gold. He was an elderly man with a shaved head, and was dressed in a long flowing skirt, with a white sash wrapped around his chest and shoulders. Despite his advanced age he was a man of vigor and had a confident heart. He honored my father at the mention of his name and praised his loyalty.

"Those times of adversity helped us recognize men of good will like your father," he said. Then he murmured a few compliments regarding my endeavor and continued, "We have destroyed the walls with all the false inscriptions they bore. The truth, however, must be recorded." He leaned his head forward in gratitude. "Now Amun sits prosperously on his throne and in the holy of holies, master of all deities, protecting Egypt and fighting off its enemies. His priests, too, have regained their precedence. Amun liberated our valley by the power he vested in Ahmose, and extended our empire in every direction by the power he vested in Tuthmosis III. For he grants victory to whom he wishes, and humbles those who betray him."

I knelt in reverence until he called on me to rise and be seated on a chair before him. I listened carefully as the high priest spoke.

———

It is a very sad story, Meriamun, though in the beginning it seemed merely an innocent whisper. It started with the

Great Queen Tiye, the heretic's mother and wife of the Great Pharaoh, Amenhotep III. She came from a common Nubian family, with not a drop of royal blood in her veins. Yet she was shrewd and powerful, as though she had four eyes and could see in all directions at once. She was intent on maintaining friendly relations with us. I shall never forget her words on the day of the Nile Festival: "You priests of Amun are the fortune and blessing of Egypt." She was so strong that she could stare with her beautiful, big eyes into the faces of powerful men till they lowered their gaze in embarrassment. We, however, did not regard her with apprehension, for we knew how the pharaohs of this glorious family had always cherished and supported the priests of Amun. Then the queen declared an interest in broadening the scope of theological doctrine to encompass other deities, and in particular Aten. On one level it appeared as a mere expansion in the knowledge of religions that we all respected and held sacred. There was no sense in protesting, although we were displeased that other deities should attain such merit here in Thebes, the home of Amun. Tiye assured us that Amun would forever remain the master of all deities, and that his priests would rank above all others in Egypt. But her words did not appease us.

One day Toto, the chanter priest, said to me, "I detect behind the queen's decision a new policy that has nothing to do with religion." When I queried his statement, he continued, "The Great Queen is seeking the sympathy of the provincial priesthood in order to curb us, limit our power, and strengthen that of the sovereign."

"But we are the servants of Amun, and in the service

of the people. We are the teachers, the healers, and the guides in this world and the hereafter. The queen is a wise woman; she must acknowledge our merits," I replied.

"But this is a power struggle. The queen is ambitious. In my opinion she is more powerful than the king," he said irritably.

"But we are the sons of the greatest deity. We are backed by a heritage stronger than destiny," I argued, against my own misgivings.

Maybe at this point I should tell you about King Amenhotep III. His grandfather, Tuthmosis III, had established an empire that surpassed all others in its vastness and the multitude of its peoples. Amenhotep III was a powerful king. He rose to the defense of his country at the slightest alarm, and achieved such triumphs that the whole empire gave him allegiance. Peace and wealth prevailed throughout his long reign, and he cultivated the fruit of his forefathers' work. Crops, minerals, fabrics, and goods, everything was abundant in Egypt. He built beautiful palaces, temples, and sculptures. He indulged himself in fine food, wine, and women, but his wife Tiye knew his strengths and weaknesses, and used them to good effect. She encouraged him to fight at times of war, and tolerated his philandering, sacrificing her feminine emotions in order to share his throne and pursue her boundless ambition. I do not deny her the merit of knowing every detail of the empire's affairs. Nor do I question her loyalty and farsightedness, or her concern for the glory of Egypt. But I do condemn her greed for power. It was greed that tempted her to exploit religion to attain exclusive power for the throne, and marginalize the priests. Gradually I became aware of other ideas that occupied her mind. One day she came to the temple, and after making her offering to Amun, preceded me with firm stride to the reception hall. As soon as we were seated she asked, "What is it that worries you?"

Before I could think of an answer, she continued quickly. "Like the priests I can read what is buried deep in people's hearts. You suspect that I have raised the status of other priests to the disadvantage of the priests of Amun."

"The priests of Amun are loyal subjects of your glorious family," I replied.

"Here is what I think," she said, her eyes glaring as she continued. "Amun is the master of all deities in Egypt. For our citizens in the empire, he is a symbol of power. They fear him. But Aten shines for everyone. He is the sun god, and anyone can embrace him."

I wondered if she was sincere, or whether it was just another pretense masking her desire to neutralize our power. In any case, I was not convinced by the argument itself.

"Your Highness," I said, "those savages must be ruled by force, not compassion."

"By compassion, too," she replied with a smile. "What is appropriate for a wild beast is not always suitable for the tamed animal."

This seemed to me a futile, womanish concept that might very well have disastrous consequences. And I was proven right by the painful events that followed.

The high priest was silent for a while as he gathered his thoughts. Then he continued.

At the beginning of her marriage, Tiye faced some difficulties. She remained childless for a considerable time, and feared she might be barren, particularly since she came from a common family. But, by the virtue of Amun and his priests, our good prayers and effective sorcery, the queen became pregnant. Even then, she gave birth to a girl. Whenever I met her in the palace or the temple, she would look at me with wariness and suspicion, as though I was responsible for her misfortune. We would never have thought of disturbing the order of the throne. It was the queen's own wickedness that made her so distrustful.

Once more he was silent, as though reluctant to continue. Then he said, "Then, in some mysterious way, she bore two sons." He thought a while, setting my curious soul on fire. "The older and better of the two passed away, while the other remained to exercise his perversity in the destruction of Egypt." I said nothing, but the high priest noticed my eagerness and went on.

We have ways of hunting out the truth even when it is hidden from others. We have the power of sorcery, and our eyes are everywhere in the empire. The heretic was a man of questionable birth, effeminate and grotesque. Following in the footsteps of his father, Amenhotep III, he married a common girl. Nefertiti was like his mother, not only in humble descent, but also in her insatiable ambition and lust. She was beautiful, stubborn, and defiant. She plunged into the affairs of the country, supporting her husband's destructive policy. She bore six girls, the fruit of her liaisons with other men. Despite his apparent love for Nefertiti, Akhenaten never really loved anyone but his mother, who gave him life and nurtured his absurd ideas. He sensed Tiye's pain and loneliness, and harbored rage against his father. When Amenhotep III died, Akhenaten erased his name from all the monuments. He said he meant to erase the name of Amun from the people's memory, and to do that his father's name—Amenhotep, meaning Amun is Content—had also to be erased. The truth is, having failed to avenge himself during his father's life, he killed him after his death. When Tiye taught him the religion of Aten, it was merely a political maneuver. But the boy believed in it as an end in itself. Politics did not befit his feminine nature. What happened next was something even his mother had not anticipated. He became a heretic.

I still remember his repulsive appearance, neither man nor woman. Because he was so weak and frail, he naturally became resentful of all strong men, priests, and deities. He conceived of a god similar to himself in weakness and femininity, both father and mother, with no other purpose but love. A god worshiped with rituals of dance and song! Akhenaten drowned in a swamp of foolishness, and neglected his obligations to the throne, while our men and loyal allies were béing massacred by the enemies of the empire. Though they cried for help, they received none, and eventually the empire was lost, Egypt was destroyed, the temples were empty, and the people famished. That was the heretic who called himself Akhenaten.

———

Overwhelmed by the intensity of his memories, the high priest was silent for a while. I waited patiently, until at last he laced his fingers and rested his hands in his lap.

———

I first received reports about Akhenaten when he was still a young boy. I had my eyes in the palace, men who had dedicated themselves to the service of Amun and the country. They told me that the crown prince nurtured a suspicious affinity for Aten, favoring him over Amun, master of all deities. I learned that every day at dawn the boy went to a secluded spot on the Nile bank to greet the sunrise in solitude. I foresaw in his strange practices a future laden with trouble. I went to the palace, where I confessed my fears to the king and queen.

"My son is still young," Amenhotep III smiled.

"But the young boy will grow, and he will retain within him the ideas of his childhood."

"He is but an innocent child seeking wisdom wherever he thinks he might find it," Tiye said.

"Soon he will begin his military training and learn his true calling," the pharaoh added.

"We have no need of more countries to add to our empire. What we need is the wisdom to keep what we already have," Tiye said.

"My glorious Queen," I argued, "the safety of the empire relies on the blessings of Amun and the exercise of power."

"I am surprised that a wise man like yourself should undervalue the role of wisdom in such a manner," said the cunning queen.

"I do not deny the importance of wisdom," I insisted, "but without power, wisdom is nothing but chatter."

"In this palace," the pharaoh interjected, "there is no question that Amun is the master of all deities."

"But the prince has stopped visiting the temple," I said anxiously.

"Be patient," the king replied. "Soon my son will fulfill all his obligations as crown prince."

I returned from the palace with no solace. Indeed, after hearing the king and queen come to the prince's defense, my fears were even stronger. Then I heard about a conversation the crown prince had with his parents and I became convinced that within the prince's frail body was an abyss of evil power. One day one of my men asked to see me. "Even the sun is no longer a god," he said. I queried him and he continued, "There are rumors that a new god has revealed himself to the crown prince, claiming to be the one and only true god and that all other deities are spurious."

The news stunned me. The fate of the older brother who died was more merciful than the madness that had descended upon the crown prince. The tragedy had reached its climax.

"Are you certain of what you say?"

"I am merely reporting what everyone says."

"How did this so-called god reveal himself to the prince?"

"He heard his voice."

"No sun? No star? No idols?"

"Nothing at all."

"How can he worship what he cannot see?"

"He believes that his god is the only power capable of creation."

"He has lost his mind."

The chanter priest, Toto, said, "The prince has gone mad and is no longer fit to take the throne when the time comes."

"Quiet," I said. "That the prince is an infidel does not change the fact that Amun and our gods will remain the only deities worshiped by the people in the empire."

"How can a heretic take the throne and rule the empire?" Toto asked angrily.

"Let us not be hasty. We will wait until the truth is clear, then we will discuss the matter with the king," I continued, my heart heavy with gloom. "It will be the first confrontation of its kind in history."

When the crown prince married Nefertiti, the eldest

daughter of the sage Ay, I held by the last of all hopes—that in marriage, the prince would return to his senses. I summoned Ay to the temple. As we talked, it became clear to me that the sage was extremely cautious in what he said. He was certainly in a predicament, and I sympathized with him, saying nothing about the prince's unbelief. Before he left, I asked him to arrange for me a private conference with his daughter.

Nefertiti arrived promptly. I looked at her keenly, and saw beyond her captivating beauty a roaring torrent of strength and power. I was instantly reminded of the Great Queen Tiye, and hoped this power would work with us and not against us.

"I grant you my blessing, my daughter."

She expressed her gratitude in a sweet, pleasing voice.

"I have no doubt that you are fully aware of your duties as the wife of the crown prince. But it is also my duty to remind you that the throne of the empire is founded on three fundamentals: Amun, the master of all deities; the pharaoh; and the queen."

"Indeed. I am fortunate to be granted the honor of your wisdom."

"A sensible queen must bear with the king the burden of protecting the empire."

"Dear Holy Priest," she said firmly, "my heart is filled with love and loyalty."

"Egypt is a country of timeless traditions, and women are the sacred guardians of this heritage."

"Duty, too, dwells within me."

Nefertiti remained wary and reserved throughout her

visit. She spoke, but revealed nothing. She was like a mysterious carving with no inscription to explain it. I could extract no information from her words, nor could I express my fears directly. Yet her wariness meant that she knew everything and that she was not on our side. Her position did not surprise me in the least. By a stroke of luck capable of turning the strongest head in the country Nefertiti had found herself a future queen. Her primary concern was neither Amun nor indeed any of the deities—she craved only the power of the throne. I said a prayer of mourning with the other priests in the holy of holies, then related to them the proceedings of my meeting with Nefertiti.

"Soon there will be nothing but darkness," said Toto the chanter. When all the other priests had left, Toto said, "Perhaps you can discuss the matter with Chief Commander Mae."

"Toto," I replied earnestly, recognizing the danger in his allusion, "we cannot defy King Amenhotep III and the Great Queen Tiye."

Meanwhile in the palace, tension was rising between the mad prince and his parents. Thus King Amenhotep III issued an imperial mandate ordering the crown prince to tour the vast empire. Perhaps the pharaoh had hoped that when the prince became acquainted with his country and subjects he would see the reality of things and realize how far he had strayed from the right path. I was grateful for the king's attempt, but my deep fears continued to haunt me. Then, while the prince was still away, some grave events took place. First, Queen Tiye gave birth to twins, Smenkhkare and Tutankhamun. Shortly after, the pharaoh's health deteriorated, and he died. Messengers from the palace carried the news to the prince, for him to return and take the throne.

I discussed the future of the country with the priests of Amun, and we came to an agreement. Immediately I took action, and asked to meet the queen despite the mourning and her preoccupation with mummifying her husband's body. Even in her grief, the queen was powerful and enduring. I was determined to speak out at any cost.

"My Queen, I came to speak my mind to the rightful matriarch of the empire." I could tell by the way she looked at me that she knew what I was about to say. "My gracious Queen, it is well known now that the crown prince does not respect our deities."

"Do not believe everything you hear," she replied.

"I am prepared to believe all that you say, Your Majesty," I said readily.

"He is a poet," she said. I was not satisfied with her answer but remained silent until she added, firmly, "He will fulfill all his duties."

I mustered up all the courage I had within me and said, "My Queen is surely aware of the consequences that would befall the throne if the gods were offended."

"Your fears are unfounded," she replied irritably.

"If necessity calls we can entrust the throne to one of your younger sons; you will be the guardian regent."

"Amenhotep IV will rule the empire. He is the crown prince."

Thus did the wise queen yield to the mother and lover

in her. She wasted the last chance for reparation, and armed destiny with the weapon that dealt us a fatal blow. The mad, effeminate crown prince returned in time for the royal entombment.

Soon afterward, I was summoned to appear before him in his formal capacity as the future pharaoh. It was the first time I had seen him closely. He was rather dark, with dreamy eyes and a thin, frail figure, noticeably feminine. His features were grotesque and disturbing. He was a despicable creature, unworthy of the throne, so weak he could not challenge an insect, let alone the Master Deity. I was disgusted but revealed nothing; instead I called to mind the words of wise men and great poets, words that inspired me to keep my patience. He fixed his gaze on me, a look neither hostile nor friendly.

I was so distracted by his appearance that I could not utter a word.

"I have had so many tedious arguments with my parents because of you," he began.

I was finally able to speak. "My only concern in this life," I said, "is the service of Amun, the throne, and the empire."

"You have something to tell me, no doubt," he said.

"My King," I replied, anticipating a battle, "I heard disturbing news, but I did not believe it."

"What you heard is the truth," he said, seemingly quite unconcerned. I was startled, but he continued, "I am the only man of faith in this heathen country."

"I cannot believe what I hear."

"You must believe it. There is no god but the One and Only God."

"Amun will not forgive this blasphemy." I was so enraged that I no longer cared about the consequences of what I said; my only concern was to defend Amun and our deities.

"No one but the One and Only God can grant forgiveness," he replied, smiling.

"Nonsense!" I said, shuddering with anger.

"He is the whole meaning of this world. He is the creator. He is the power. He is love, peace, and happiness." Then he threw me a piercing look that seemed out of keeping with his fragile appearance, and continued, "I call upon you to believe in him."

"Beware of the wrath of Amun," I said furiously. "He creates, and He destroys. He grants and dispossesses, aids and forsakes. Fear his vengeance for it shall haunt you to your last descendant, and destroy your throne and the empire."

"I am but a child in the vast expanse of the One and Only, a budding flower in his garden, and a servant at his command. He granted me his gracious love and revealed himself to my soul. He filled me with brilliant light and beautiful music. That is all that matters to me."

"A prince does not become a pharaoh until he is crowned in the temple of Amun."

"I shall be crowned in the open land under the sunlight, with the blessing of the creator."

We parted on the poorest terms. On my side there was Amun and his followers. Akhenaten had the heritage of his great family, the holiness with which the subjects regarded their pharaohs, and his madness. I prepared myself for holy war, and was ready to sacrifice everything for the sake of Amun and my country. I put myself to work without delay.

"The new pharaoh is a heretic," I told the priests. "You must know that, and let everyone in the country be informed."

I too was furious, but I thought it best to channel Toto's anger. I proposed that he should pretend to join the heretic, to become our eyes in the palace. As for the king, he, too, lost no time. He was crowned with the blessings of his so-called god. He even built a temple for him in Thebes, the city of Amun. He proclaimed his new religion to the candidates for his chamber, and consequently the finest men of Egypt declared their faith in the new god. Their particular motives may have varied, but the goal was one—to fulfill their ambition and attain power. Perhaps if they had renounced his religion, things would have taken a different course. But they sold themselves like whores. Take the sage Ay, for instance. He thought himself a part of the pharaoh's family and was blinded by glory. Haremhab, a courageous warrior, was another one. He was a man of no true faith; for him it was simply a matter of substituting one name for another. All the others, too, they were nothing but a band of hypocrites, hungry for wealth and power. Had they not renounced their sinful ways and repented at the critical moment, they would have deserved to die. In the event, they won their lives back, but I have no respect for any of them.

The conflict threatened Thebes. People were torn between their loyalty to Amun and their obligation to the mad offshoot of the greatest family in our history.

The Great Queen Tiye was consumed with worry as she watched the seed she had sown grow into a poisonous plant. He was falling into a bottomless pit, dragging his family along with him. Tiye kept bringing her offerings to the temple of Amun, in an attempt to diminish the turmoil that jeopardized the throne.

"You win by allegiance, and lose by defiance," she said.

"You are asking us to be loyal to a heretic. If only you had listened to me in the beginning."

"We must not despair."

Her usual strength collapsed in the face of his mysterious insanity, and she was impotent before her effeminate, spoilt son. It was inevitable that we continue our holy struggle. The mad king was no longer able to bear the pressure in Thebes, particularly when he heard the hostile cries of the people during the feast of Amun. Claiming that his god had commanded him to leave Thebes and build a new city, he left in a grand exodus with eighty thousand other heretics, to live in their accursed exile. His move from Thebes gave us time to prepare for holy war, and allowed him to indulge his blasphemy and make the new capital a place for riotous festivities and orgies. Love and Joy, this was the slogan of his new, nameless god. Whenever his natural weakness stung him, he went to extremes to prove that his power had no limits. The priests were evicted and the temples closed. The idols and all the patrimonial endowments were confiscated. I said to the priests, "It is death and the hereafter you must cherish, for there is nothing to live for now that the temples are closed." But we found refuge in the homes of the pious followers of Amun. They were our fighters, and we continued the struggle with hope and determination.

The heretic continued to flaunt his power, parading in the provinces and calling upon the people to join him in his heresy. Those were the darkest days. The people were torn and dismayed, not knowing whether to choose their deities or their feeble king and his obscenely beautiful wife. Those were the days of grief and torment, hypocrisy and regret, and fear of divine wrath. But the words of love and joy began to take their toll. The public servants cared little for their duties and exploited citizens for their pleasure. Rebellion spread throughout the empire. Our enemies feared us no more, and began to threaten our borders. When the rulers in the provinces called for help they received poems instead of troops. They died as martyrs, cursing the treacherous heretic with their final breath. The stream of riches that had flown into Egypt from all over the world dried up, leaving the markets bare, the merchants impoverished, and the country famished. I cried out to the people, "The curse of Amun has descended upon us. We must destroy the heretic, or else we will be extinguished in war."

Still I opted for the path of peace to spare the country the trauma of war. I confronted the queen mother, Tiye.

"I am troubled and grieved, High Priest of Amun," she said.

"I am no longer high priest." Bitterness grasped me. "I am only a hunted vagabond now."

"I ask the gods for mercy," she stuttered.

"You must do something. He is your son; he adores you. You are responsible for all that has happened. Caution him before a civil war wipes out everything."

She was vexed when I reminded her of her responsibility. She said, "I have decided to go to the new capital, Akhetaten."

Indeed Queen Tiye made some deserving efforts, but she could not repair the damage. I did not despair, but went to Akhetaten, despite the danger in such an undertaking. There I met with the heretic's men.

"I speak to you from a position of power," I said. "My men are awaiting a signal from me to pounce on you. I am here now in a last attempt to save what can possibly be saved without bloodshed or destruction. I will leave you to yourselves for a while, and trust you will come to your senses and do your duty."

They appeared to be convinced, and in due time they did what I asked of them, each for his own purposes. But the country was spared grave affliction. They met with the heretic and presented him with two urgent demands—to declare freedom of worship, and to send an army to defend the empire against our enemies who were making incursions across the borders. The mad king refused. They proposed that if he abdicated the throne, he could keep his faith and preach it however he wished. Again, their offer was rejected. But this time he appointed his brother Smenkhkare to share the throne. We disregarded his order and named Tutankhamun king of the throne. The heretic's men deserted him and pledged allegiance to the new pharaoh. In time, order was restored in the country without war or destruction. We relinquished all desire for revenge on the madman and his wife and those who remained loyal to him.

Amun's followers hurried to the temples after their long deprivation. The nightmare had ended and life began to resume its normal course. As for the heretic, when madness had consumed him, he fell ill and died, disappointed in his god and hopeless of the hereafter. He left behind him his wicked wife to endure loneliness and regret.

———

The high priest gazed at me silently for a long while. Then he said, "We are still healing. We need time and serious effort. Our loss, inside and outside the empire, was beyond estimate. How did it all happen? How could such a mad, distorted person stir up such agony?" He paused for a moment then concluded, "That is the true story. Record it faithfully. Do carry my sincere greetings to your dear father."

Ay

————

Ay was the sage and former counselor to Akhenaten, and father of Nefertiti and Mutnedjmet. Old age had settled in the furrows of his face. I met him in his palace overlooking the Nile in south Thebes. He told me the story in a serene voice without letting his face reveal any emotion. I was in awe of his solemnity and dignity, and the richness of his experience. "Life, Meriamun, is a wonder," he began. "It is a sky laden with clouds of contradictions." He contemplated a while, surrendering to a current of memories. Then, he continued.

————

The story begins one summer day when I was summoned to appear before King Amenhotep III and Great Queen Tiye.

"You are a wise man, Ay," the queen said. "Your knowledge of the secular and the spiritual is unrivaled.

We have decided to entrust you with the education of our sons Tuthmosis and Amenhotep."

I bowed my shaven head in gratitude and said, "Fortunate is he who will have the honor of serving the king and queen."

Tuthmosis was seven years old, Amenhotep was six. Tuthmosis was strong, handsome, and well built, though not particularly tall. Amenhotep was dark, tall, and slender, with small, feminine features. He had a tender yet penetrating look that made a deep impression on me. The handsome lad died and the weak one was spared. The death of his brother shook Amenhotep and he wept for a long time.

One day he said to me, "Master, my brother was pious, he frequented the temple of Amun, received his charms and fetishes, but still he was left to die. Master and Sage, why don't you bring him back to life?"

"Son," I replied, "one's soul is immortal. Let that be your solace."

That was the beginning of our many discussions on life and death. I was sincerely pleased with his insight and understanding in spiritual matters. The boy was clearly ahead of his years. I often found myself thinking that Akhenaten was born with some otherworldly wisdom. Even in secular subjects, he quickly mastered the skills of reading, writing, and algebra. I said to Queen Tiye, "His abilities are so extraordinary that he is beginning to intimidate his master."

I looked forward to lessons with him and wondered what his mind would produce when he reigned over the

empire of his forefathers. I was certain that the greatness
of his empire would surpass that of his father's.

Amenhotep III was a great and powerful ruler. He
was merciless with his enemies and those who disobeyed
him. In peaceful times he indulged himself with women,
food, and wine. He became so thoroughly consumed by
those pleasures that he soon fell victim to all kinds of ail-
ments, and spent his last days in agony, suffering excru-
ciating pains. As for Queen Tiye, she came from an
honorable Nubian family. She proved to be a woman of
such power and wisdom that she outshone even Queen
Hatshepsut. Because of the death of her eldest son and
her husband's infidelity she became very attached to the
young Amenhotep. It was as if she were his mother, his
lover, and his teacher. She was so passionate about politics that she sacrificed her feminine heart to nourish her
ambition for power. The priests falsely accused her of
being responsible for her son's perversity. The truth is
that she wanted him to be abreast of all religions. Perhaps she wanted Aten to replace Amun and become the
deity to whom all others owed allegiance, for Aten
was the sun god who breathed life everywhere. His subjects were united by faith and not merely by force.
She hoped to use religion as a political instrument that
could bring about the unity of Egypt. It was not her
intention that her son believe in the religion and not
the politics, but Akhenaten refused to put religion in
the service of anything. The mother had contrived a
clever political scheme, but the son believed in the
means, not the end. He devoted himself to his religious

calling, jeopardizing the country, the empire, and the throne.

––––––––

Ay remained silent for a while. He tightened the sash around his shoulders. His face looked rather small under the thick wig. When some time had passed in silence, he continued.

––––––––

I am still amazed at the young boy's intelligence. It was as if he had been born with the mind of a high priest. I often caught myself arguing with him as though he were my equal. By the time he was ten, his mind was like a hot spring, sparkling with ideas. His weak body harbored such a strong will and perseverance that I took him as living proof that the human spirit could be stronger than the most exercised muscles. He was so devoted to his religious instruction that he spent no time preparing himself for the throne. He would not accept any idea without questioning and argument, and he never hesitated to express his doubts about many of our traditional teachings. I was taken aback when, one time, he said, "Thebes! A holy city! Isn't that what they claim? Thebes, Master, is nothing but a den of rapacious merchants, debauchery, and fornication. Who are those great priests? They delude people with superstition, and take from the poor what little they have. They seduce women in the name of the deities. Their temple has become a house of harlotry and sin. Accursed Thebes."

I was greatly concerned when I heard him speak these

words. I could see accusing fingers pointed at me, his teacher.

"Those priests are the foundation of the throne," I replied.

"Then the throne is built on lies and dissolution."

"Their power is no less than that of an army," I warned him.

"Bandits and thugs are powerful, too."

It was clear from the very beginning that he disliked Amun, who reigned in the holy of holies. He favored Aten, whose light shone throughout the world.

"Amun is the god of priests, but Aten is God of heaven and earth."

"You should be loyal to all deities."

"Should I not trust my heart to show me the difference between right and wrong?" he asked.

"One day you will be crowned in the temple of Amun," I said in an attempt to persuade him.

He spread his slender arms and said, "I would rather be crowned in the open air, under the light of the sun."

"Amun is the deity that empowered your ancestors and gave them victory over their enemies."

He remained quiet, thinking, then said, "I cannot understand how a god could allow anyone to massacre his own creation."

I grew more worried but continued my efforts to dissuade him. "But we, the subjects of Amun, cannot always understand his holy wisdom."

"The sunlight of Aten does not discriminate between people when it shines down upon us."

"You must not forget that life is a battleground."

"Master," he replied sadly, "do not speak to me of war. Have you not seen the sun when it rises above the fields and the Nile? Have you not seen the horizon when the sun goes down? Have you heard the nightingale sing, or the doves coo? Have you never felt the sacred happiness buried deep in your heart?"

I knew that there was nothing I could do. He was like a tree and I could not stop him from growing. I conveyed my fears to the queen, but she did not share my concerns.

"He is still an innocent child, Ay," she said. "He will learn more of this life as he grows. Soon he will begin his military training."

The pious young prince started his military training along with the sons of the nobles. He detested it, possibly because of his physical weakness. Soon he rejected the training, thus admitting a failure not befitting a king's son.

"I do not wish to learn the fundamentals of murder," he said bitterly.

The king was saddened by his son's decision. "A king who cannot fight is at the mercy of his commanders," he said.

The crown prince and the king had several confrontations. Most likely, this strife was the seed of the malice the boy harbored against his great father. I do believe, however, that the priests of Amun stretched this fact when they accused him of avenging himself by erasing his father's name from all the monuments. He only wanted to eradicate the name of Amun. He even changed his own name from Amenhotep to Akhenaten for the same purpose. Then came the night that condemned him to a life of seclusion. He had been waiting for the sunrise in the dark royal garden by the bank of the Nile. I learned all the details when I met him in the morning. I believe it was spring time. The air was clear of all dew and dust. When I greeted him, he turned to me with a pale face and mesmerized eyes.

"Master, the truth has been revealed to me," he said without returning my greeting. "I came here before sunrise. The night was my companion, its silence my blessing. As I bid darkness farewell, I felt that I was rising with the air around me. It was as though I was retreating with the night. Then there was a marvelous light, and I saw all the creatures that I had seen or even heard of gather before my eyes and greet each other in delight. I had overcome pain and death, I thought. I was intoxicated with the sweet scent of creation. I heard his clear voice speaking to me: 'I am the One and Only God; there is no God but I. I am the truth. Dwell in my kingdom, and worship me only. Give me yourself; I have granted you my divine love.'"

We stared at each other for a long while. I was overcome by despair and could not speak.

"Do you not believe me, Master?"

"You never lie," I replied.

"Then you must believe me," he said in ecstasy.

"What did you see?"

"I only heard his voice in the merry dawn."

"My son," I hesitated, "if you saw nothing, that means there was nothing."

"This is how he reveals himself," he replied firmly.

"Perhaps it was Aten."

"No. Not Aten, not the sun. He is above and beyond that. He is the One and Only God."

I was mystified. "Where do you worship him?"

"Anywhere, anytime. He will give me the strength and love to worship him."

———

Ay was silent. I wanted to ask him if he believed in Akhenaten's god, but I remembered my father's advice and remained silent. Ay, along with many others, had left Akhenaten when things were at their worst. Perhaps he had been forced to deny his faith for the rest of his life.

———

I had to tell the king and queen. A few days later, I found the crown prince waiting for me in his favorite part of the garden.

"You reported me as usual, Master," he smiled reproachfully.

"It is my duty," I replied calmly.

He laughed and said, "The confrontation with my father was rather interesting. When I recounted my experience to him, he grimaced and said, 'You must be examined by Bento, the physician.' I replied politely that I was in good health. 'I have yet to see a madman confess to insanity,' he said. Then he continued, this time in a threatening tone, 'The deities are the foundations of Egypt. The king must believe in all the deities of his people. This god that you spoke of is nothing. He does not deserve to join our deities.' I told him that he was the Only God; that there is no other god. 'This is heresy and madness,' he cried. I repeated that he was the One and Only God. He became extremely angry and said, 'I command you to renounce these absurd ideas, and to honor the heritage of your ancestors.' I did not say any more so as not to show him disrespect. Then my mother said, 'All we ask of you is to honor and respect a holy duty. Let your heart love what your heart wishes to love, until you return to the right path. Meanwhile, do not neglect your duty.' I left them feeling sad, but more determined."

"My dear Prince," I said earnestly, "the pharaoh is a product of ancient and holy traditions. Do not ever forget that."

From that moment, I was sure that there were troubles ahead such as Egypt had never seen or imagined before. The great family of pharaohs that had liberated the country and created an empire was now standing at the edge of an abyss. Around that time—perhaps it was earlier, I am not quite certain of the chronology—I was summoned to a closed meeting by the high priest of Amun.

"You and I have known each other for a very long time, Ay," he said. "What is all this that I hear?"

As I say, I do not recall whether this meeting took place after it became known that the prince was inclined toward Aten, or after he declared his faith in the One and Only God. In any event, I replied, "The prince is a fine, sensible young man. Only, he is still too young. At such a sensitive age, one tends to follow one's imagination indiscriminately. He will soon mature and return to the right path."

"How could he renounce the wisdom of the best teacher in the country?"

"How can one control the flow of a river during the flood season?" I said in an effort to defend myself.

"Our duty, as the elite of this country, is to put our religion and empire first."

I had endless discussions with my wife, Tey, and my daughters, Nefertiti and Mutnedjmet, trying to make sense of the confusion that rattled in my mind day and night. Tey and Mutnedjmet accused the prince of heresy. Nefertiti, on the other hand, had no qualms about supporting him. Indeed she liked his ideas. "He speaks the truth, Father," she whispered. Nefertiti was about the same age as Akhenaten and, like the prince, had matured beyond her years. Both girls had completed their basic education and home-making training. Mutnedjmet was good at writing and recitation, algebra, embroidery, sewing, cooking, painting, and ritual dance. Nefertiti excelled in the same subjects, but was not content with them. She developed a strong interest in theology and logic. I noticed her fondness for Aten, and later, when she declared her faith in the One God, I was aghast. "He is the only god able to rescue me from the torture of confusion," she announced.

Tey and Mutnedjmet were furious, and accused her of apostasy.

At that time, we were invited to the pharaoh's palace

to celebrate thirty years of his reign. It was the first time our daughters had entered the palace, and by a stroke of fate, Nefertiti won the love of the crown prince. Everything happened so quickly thereafter. We could still hardly believe it, when Nefertiti and Akhenaten became husband and wife. I was summoned once more by the high priest of Amun. This time, as I stood before him, I felt that he regarded me as a potential enemy.

"You have become a member of the royalty, Ay." His voice was filled with apprehension.

"I am but a man who has never strayed from the course of duty."

"Only time can prove the true merits of men," he said calmly.

He asked me to arrange for a conference with Nefertiti. Before the appointed time I spoke with my daughter and armed her with advice. I must say though that Nefertiti had no need of counseling—her own wisdom aided her more than any advice she received. She answered the high priest's questions eloquently, without revealing secrets or making commitments. I believe that the priest's hostility toward my daughter started with that encounter.

"Father," she reported, "it may have seemed an innocent meeting on the surface, but in reality we were fighting an undeclared war. He claims that he is concerned for the empire when in fact he is only worried about his share of the goods that flow into the temple. He is a crafty, wicked man."

When the conflict grew between the pharaoh and his son, the king called me in and said, "I think we should send the prince on a tour of the empire. He needs experience, and must learn more about people and life." At that time, the king was enjoying his last days with a bride young enough to be his granddaughter—Tadukhipa, daughter of Tushratta, the king of Mitanni.

"It is a sound idea, my gracious King," I replied sincerely.

So Akhenaten left Thebes accompanied by a delegation of the best young men in the country. I, too, was chosen to go with him on that memorable journey. In the provinces, the subjects had expected to see a powerful, invincible being, a high and mighty god looking down upon them. Instead, the crown prince greeted them humbly as he walked among them in public gardens and on their plantations. Priests and religious scholars were invited to convene with him. He denounced their faiths. What god, he asked, is so bloodthirsty that it cannot be worshiped without the sacrifice of human souls? He proclaimed his One God the only creator of the universe. He told them that God regarded all his creation indiscriminately with love, peace, and joy; that love was the only law, peace was the ultimate end, and joy was the gratitude offered to the creator. Everywhere he went he left behind a whirlwind of confusion and frenzied excitement. I became extremely alarmed.

"My dear Prince," I said, "you are pulling out the roots of the empire."

He laughed. "When will you believe, Master?"

"You have slandered all the religions of our ancestors, religions we have learned to believe in and respect. Equality . . . love . . . peace . . . all this means nothing to the subjects but an open invitation to rebelliousness and strife."

He thought a while, then asked, "Why do wise men like yourself believe so firmly in evil?"

"We believe in reality."

"Master," he said with a smile, "I will forever dwell in truth."

Before we were able to visit all the provinces as planned, a messenger from the palace reached us with the news that the Great Pharaoh was dead.

———

Ay recounted the details of their return to Thebes, the grand entombment ceremony, and the crowning of the prince on the throne of Egypt. Akhenaten became King Amenhotep IV, and his wife, Nefertiti, the Great Queen. As was the custom, the new king inherited his father's harem. Although he treated them kindly, he abstained from any pleasure they offered him.

Ay then told me how Akhenaten summoned the noble men of the country and urged them to join his religion. Thus, he was able to select his men from those who declared their faith in the One and Only God. Mae was appointed commander of the armed forces; Haremhab became chief of security; Ay was chosen for the position of adviser to the throne.

"You will hear conflicting reports on why we declared our faith in Akhenaten's god," Ay told me. "But no one knows what the heart really holds." Feeling that I was after the secret of his heart, he told me, "I believed in the new god as a deity to be worshiped along with all the other deities. But I also believed that everyone should have the freedom to worship whichever god they chose."

Akhenaten continued his reform throughout the empire. He reduced taxes, and abolished all punitive measures. "My King," Ay advised him, "if public servants are no longer afraid of punishment, they will soon become corrupt, and the poor will be their sorry prey." The king shrugged and replied confidently, "You are still wavering, Ay, and your faith is not strong enough. You will soon see what wonders love can do. My God will never let me down." Meanwhile, relations between the new king and the priests of Amun had become so strained that Akhenaten resolved to build a new city and move the throne.

Thus we moved to Akhetaten, a city of unrivaled beauty. Upon arrival, we held the first prayer in the grand temple that was erected in the center of the city. Nefertiti played the mandolin. She was like a jewel, radiant with youth and beauty as she sang:

> O Precious Lord, Sole Creator,
> You fill the universe with thy beauty.
> There is no love greater than thine.

Each passing day was a sweet dream, filled with happiness and love. The blossom of the new religion was growing rapidly in our hearts. But the king did not forget his mission. In the name of love and peace, the pharaoh fought the most ferocious war Egypt had witnessed. He decreed the closing of temples, confiscated all the idols, and erased their names from the monuments. It was then that he changed his name to Akhenaten. Then he toured the country proclaiming his religion. People received him with amazing love and eagerness. In the past, they had heard about pharaohs without ever seeing them, but now the image of Akhenaten and Nefertiti in their public appearances became engraved on their memories forever.

But the dream did not last. Clouds of sorrow began to gather; hesitant at first, then quickly they broke like a fierce cataract. There was the death of his second daughter, Meketaten, the most beautiful and loved one of all his children. He was consumed with grief, and mourned her with more tears than he had shed in his boyhood after the death of his brother Tuthmosis.

When he cried out "Why?" to his god, I suspected he was about to lose his faith. Then we began to receive news of the growing corruption of the public servants and merchants. The cries of hungry people grew louder. Several regions of the empire were now in a state of mutiny. Our enemies began to attack the borders. Tushratta, king of Mitanni and our strongest ally, was killed defending the country.

"We must eradicate all the elements of corruption, and send the army to defend our borders," I urged him desperately.

"Love is my arms and my armor, Ay," he said, unwavering. "You must be patient."

How can I possibly explain the curious events that transpired? The priests accused the pharaoh of madness. In his last days, some of Akhenaten's men came to share that opinion. Although I was admittedly rather confused, I rejected that idea completely. He was neither mad nor sane like the rest of us. He was something in between. I could never understand him.

The queen mother, Tiye, sent word that she was preparing to visit Akhetaten. Akhenaten was so pleased that he built a palace in the southern quarter of the city specially for the occasion, and the reception held in her honor was the most magnificent celebration the city had witnessed. Shortly after her arrival, Tiye asked to see me. It amazed me to see how she had aged beyond her years.

"Ay," she started, "I came to have a very long talk with my son. But I thought it appropriate to pave the way by consulting you first."

"I have never neglected my duty as a reliable adviser," I replied.

"I believe you," she continued. "Ay, I agree that we must never let go of our heritage. But I want you to tell me in all honesty, will you remain loyal to my son regardless of what happens?"

"You must never doubt that," I replied earnestly.

"What would you do should something arise that relieves you of your duty to the king?"

"I am a member of his family. I would never abandon him."

"I am grateful, Ay," the Great Queen sighed in relief. "The situation is rather dangerous. Do you think the others have such strong faith in him as well?"

I thought for a while then replied, "I can assure you that some of them, at least, are beyond doubt."

"I am particularly curious to hear what you have to say about Haremhab." She seemed apprehensive.

"He is faithful in his duties as chief of security, and has been a friend of the king since they were young lads," I replied without hesitation.

"It is him who worries me the most."

"Perhaps because of the great power at his command. In truth, however, he is as loyal to the king as Meri-Ra."

Like the rest of us, Tiye failed to sway the king from his position. Eventually, she packed her disappointment and returned to Thebes. There, her health deteriorated quickly and she passed away, leaving behind the tales of her wonderful life.

Resentment escalated in the empire and all the provinces now turned against the king. We became imprisoned in Akhetaten with our One and Only God. We were all aware of the impending disaster. Except Akhenaten, who was still hopeful. "My God will never forsake me," he insisted.

Unbeknown to anyone, the high priest of Amun entered Akhetaten. When I learned that he was in the city, I was one of the first to visit him. I was surprised to find him disguised in the garb of a merchant.

"You wish to conceal your identity? Why, you know that the king brings no harm upon anyone."

He ignored my question and commanded, "Gather all the king's men and bring them to me."

We met with him in the garden of the palace of the late Queen Tiye. He asked us to collaborate with him to avoid bloodshed. He seemed to be speaking to us from a position of power. He talked at length about the wrath of the gods and the fate of the empire. Then he delivered us a severe warning and left. We felt as though a snake had just brushed by our feet. I did not know how to interpret his actions; I had never trusted him in the first place. I suspected, however, that the high priest did not trust the troops in the provinces to be on his side either. He was afraid, I concluded, of a nationwide conflict that would end either in his destruction or, at best, in a very costly victory. The threat he faced was no less than that looming over Akhetaten. Nonetheless, if a civil war broke out, all of Egypt would pay the price. When the high priest left, we stayed behind to discuss the situation, hoping to come to a decision.

———

At that point I had to interrupt him. "Which of the king's men were present at that meeting?" He squinted, mulling over my question for a while, then continued.

———

I do not recall precisely. It has been a very long time. I do remember, however, that Haremhab and Nakht were there. In any case, Haremhab was the first to speak.

"I am the king's friend and chief of security," he said. He gazed at us with his honey-colored eyes for a while then continued in a calm, determined tone. "But I believe a settlement is inevitable in this situation."

None of us protested. We requested a council convention with the king.

We stood before the pharaoh and the queen, saluting the throne and the empire. Akhenaten smiled serenely. Contrary to her usual bright demeanor, Nefertiti was cold and apprehensive. When the formalities were concluded, Akhenaten said, "I see troubled faces before me."

"My gracious King," Haremhab started, "we are gathered here for the love of Egypt."

"Everything I do is for the love of Egypt and the entire world," he replied.

"The country is on the verge of an uncontrollable war. We must do something quickly to save it, before it is completely destroyed," Haremhab continued.

"What do you recommend?" the king asked.

"Grant the people freedom of worship, and send the army to defend the borders of the empire."

The king shook his head, adorned with the crown of the Two Lands, and said, "That would mean a return to the darkness of heathen ways. I have no right to issue any decrees unless the Creator commands me."

"Your Imperial Grace," Haremhab continued, "you have every right to keep your faith, but you must then renounce the throne."

"Never will I commit such treachery against my worshiped God. I will not forsake his throne." His eyes gleamed like rays of the sun. Then he shifted his gaze to me and I felt as though I had been thrown into the netherworld.

"It is the only way to protect you and your faith," I said.

"Go in peace," he said sadly.

"You have some time to reflect on our proposition."

As we left the grand hall of the throne, I felt as though needles were pricking my heart, mercilessly. That feeling has never left me to this very day.

Grave events followed our confrontation with the king. Nefertiti left the royal palace and moved to her private palace in northern Akhetaten. I visited her, not sure of her intentions. "I shall not leave my palace until death takes me." She refused to say more. Akhenaten declared his brother Smenkhkare co-ruler on the throne of the empire. The priests denied Smenkhkare and Akhenaten the throne, and entrusted it to Tutankhamun. There was no choice but to yield or to face war. At the end of the period we gave Akhenaten to consider our counsel, Haremhab visited the palace.

"I will not betray my Creator, nor will He forsake me. I will remain firm in my position even if everyone else leaves," said the pharaoh.

"My King," Haremhab said, "we ask your permission to leave Akhetaten and return to Thebes so that the country may be reunified. Not one of us wishes to leave your city, but we must if Egypt is to be spared destruction. I will see to it that you are never harmed."

"Do as you please." Akhenaten was determined, even enthusiastic. "I am in no need of anyone's protection. God is on my side and he shall not forsake me."

We carried out our orders and left Akhetaten weighed down with sadness. Soon after, the citizens did likewise, until there was no one left but Akhenaten in his palace, Nefertiti in hers, and a few guards and slaves. Akhenaten, who had never been sick since childhood, fell ill and died alone. I learned that even in the throes of death, he prayed to his god:

You create the germ of life
Within a woman, the seed of man.
You grant us the bounty of living
Before we see the light of your land.
Should you choose to cease your giving
The earth shall be in darkness,
In the silence of death.

———

Ay was silent. When he recovered from the memories that overwhelmed him, he turned toward me, his eyes filled with compassion, and said, "This is the story of Akhenaten, the pharaoh whose only name today is the heretic. I cannot deny the woes he brought upon the country. Egypt lost its empire and was torn by conflict. But I must admit I cannot rid my heart of his love, nor can I stop admiring him. Let the final word be that of Osiris, the ruler of eternal life, before whom we shall all stand to be judged."

As I left the palace of the sage, it occurred to me that the final word on Ay will not be pronounced until he, too, stands before Osiris.

Haremhab

———

Haremhab was well built, moderately tall, with a strong, trustworthy demeanor. He was a descendant of an old religious family from Memphis, a family that had produced renowned physicians, priests, and army officials. Haremhab's father was the first in his family to be elevated to the ruling class when he was appointed chief of horsemen during the life of Amenhotep III. Haremhab was the only one of Akhenaten's men who kept his position as chief of security in the new era. His main duty at that time was to eradicate the corruption that had spread in the country and to restore peace. He was so successful that in the critical period of transition from Akhenaten's rule, Haremhab was regarded as a hero. The high priest of Amun gave him a glowing testimony, and Ay, the sage, confirmed it. He received me in the visitors' hall by the palace garden.

———

Akhenaten was my companion and friend from boyhood, long before he was my king. From the time I first knew him, until we parted, he thought of nothing but religion. I gave him the respect that was due to him from the beginning, for I was raised to worship duty and to place everything in that context, regardless of any personal emotions or attachments. Akhenaten was the crown prince, I was one of his subjects. I owed him respect. In my heart, however, I despised him for his weakness and his feminine appearance. I could not picture myself a friend of his. But the fact is, he won me and I became his true friend. I still wonder how it all happened. Perhaps I was unable to resist his tender, delicate emotions and his charm. He possessed an amazing ability to capture people's hearts. He even had the entire country applaud him as he called upon them to renounce the deities of their forefathers.

Akhenaten and I were opposites. But that did not stop us from developing a very firm friendship that withstood several trials, until finally it was crushed by a mountain of contradiction. I can still see his smile as he said, "Haremhab, my bloodthirsty, monstrous friend, I love you." I searched in vain for something we might have in common. I invited him several times to join me in my favorite sport, hunting. He would always reply, "Beware and do not defile the loving heart of nature." He disliked military training, even the uniform. One time he stared at my helmet and my sword and said, "Is it not strange that decent people like yourself are trained to become professional executioners?"

"What would your great-grandfather, Tuthmosis III, say if he heard you?"

"My *great*-grandfather!" he cried. "He established his greatness on a pyramid of poor people's corpses. Did you not see his pictures on the walls of the temples? Making offerings of slaves to Amun? What great-grandfather, what bloodthirsty god?"

His strange ideas, I thought, may not stand in the way of his friendships, but what would happen if he took them to the throne? I was unable to imagine him as a pharaoh, like all the great pharaohs of Egypt. My feeling never changed, even during the merriest and most blissful times. Indeed during those times he seemed even further from the gravity and glory of the pharaohs.

Once, during his father's rule, I was deputed to discipline some rebels in a far corner of the empire. I set out in charge of an armed raid for the first time. My mission was carried out successfully and I returned with plenty of loot and captives. King Amenhotep III was impressed and honored me generously. When the prince congratulated me on my safe return, I invited him to see the captives. They stood before him shackled and half naked. As he gazed at them, their eyes begged for sympathy, as if they sensed his weakness. A cloud of gloom came over his face.

"Rest in peace," he said tenderly, "you shall not be harmed."

I became quite agitated, for I had vowed to punish them severely until they were willing to renounce chaos and submit to order.

"Haremhab," he asked as we left together, "are you proud of what you did?"

"My Prince," I replied, "I have earned this pride."

"What a pity," he mumbled, then continued teasingly, "you are just a sophisticated bandit."

That was Akhenaten, the crown prince who would in time take the throne and rule the empire. Nonetheless, I was intrigued and craved more of the strange fruit of his mind. It never affected my own ideas though. It was like listening to a voice from another world, intriguing yet incomprehensible. How did we become friends? How did my heart become filled with love for him? These are questions I cannot answer.

I recall a discussion we had about religion one time. We were resting near his private place in the palace garden.

"Haremhab," he asked, "why do you pray in the temple of Amun?"

I was taken aback. I had no answer that would satisfy him or me. I remained silent.

"Do you really believe in Amun, and all you were taught about him?"

I thought about the question for a short while then replied, "Not in the same way that other people believe in him."

"Either you believe or you do not. There is no middle way."

"I only care about religion as one of the oldest traditions in Egypt," I said in all honesty.

"You worship only yourself, Haremhab," he said with provoking confidence.

"Let us say that I worship Egypt."

"Have you ever been tempted to ask what is the secret of life and existence?"

"I know how to eliminate such temptations when they arise," I replied.

"How unfortunate. And what have you done for your soul then?"

"Duty is what I hold sacred." I was growing weary of his pressing questions. "And I have built myself a tomb for the hereafter."

He sighed. "I hope one day you will savor the sweetness of intimacy."

"Intimacy?"

"Intimacy with the one creator of the universe."

"Why one creator only?" I questioned, somewhat impassive.

"Because he is too great to have an equal," he replied serenely.

Akhenaten! A feeble shadow wandering aimlessly in the palace garden, flirting with flowers and birds, singing like a girl. I could swear he was meant to be born female, and at the last minute nature changed its course. A grave misfortune for Egypt. The first time Nefertiti made an appearance in the royal palace was in the Sed festival, the thirtieth jubilee of the pharaoh's reign. She stunned everyone with her beauty and spirit. She danced with the daughters of the honorables, and charmed us all with her sensuous voice:

O brother of mine,
Come to the sweet spring.

Watch me
As I bathe before your eyes,
My flowing robe, wet, clinging,
Lustrous under the light.
Come watch me,
Brother of mine.

Her parents, Ay and Tey, must have prepared her for such an impressive display; they had paved the way for her to sit on the throne of Egypt. Bear in mind that Ay was the crown prince's teacher. No doubt he had every chance to influence Akhenaten's shaky character, and to lead him by the hand to the snare that he had set with his daughter. In any event, Nefertiti won the affection of both the prince and his mother at the Sed festival. Not too long after, she was married to the crown prince.

During the wedding celebrations, the high priest of Amun said to me, "Perhaps in marriage the prince will mature and put aside his foolish ideas."

"A common woman like her," I replied, pointing at Nefertiti, "probably never dreamed of the throne. She will not jeopardize it by angering her husband."

I have often wondered if she would have taken him as her husband if he was not crown prince. You see, it is hard to imagine Akhenaten as the knight of any girl's dream, even if she was a simple peasant.

Marriage did not calm him. On the contrary he became more defiant. In time I learned about his peculiar claim: a new god, revealed to him through a voice and no vision. The future, I thought then, would be grim. After a while, news came that Amenhotep III was so angry with the prince that he had sent him on a long tour of the empire.

———

Haremhab went on to tell me in detail about Akhenaten's talks with the people of the empire, when he called on them to join his new religion and promised them love and joy and equal treatment. He added nothing to what I had heard from Ay.

———

Despite our friendship and my loyalty to the prince, I wished then, for the first time, to kill him with my own sword before he drowned us all in his destruction. You must understand however that my desire to kill him was not at all inspired by spite.

Amenhotep III died, and the prince was summoned to the throne. When he became pharaoh, he invited all his men to join his new religion. Then it was my turn.

"Haremhab," he said, "those who will cooperate with me must declare their faith in the One and Only."

"My dear Pharaoh, you know my position regarding all gods and religions. Nevertheless, I am a man of duty and a servant of the throne. I therefore declare my faith in the One and Only out of loyalty to your throne and to the country."

He smiled. "That should be enough for the time being. I do not wish my palace to be without you. Perhaps one day you will be blessed with true faith."

So I started a new life in the service of a new god and a new king. I served them with a loyalty drawn only from my sense of duty. But I must admit that the king revealed new powers I was not aware he possessed. Despite his physical feebleness and feminine appearance he challenged everything that came his way. He fought against the most powerful and resourceful men, the priests. He destroyed the old traditions that had been rooted in our country for hundreds of years. He even fought sorcery and potent witchcraft. Nefertiti, too, revealed herself to be a true queen, as if she had been born with the sole purpose of emulating the greatness of Tiye and Hatshepsut. She was the one who ran the affairs of the kingdom while the king devoted his time to his religious calling. Unfortunately, Nefertiti seemed to believe in the new religion. So much has been said about this woman, and I despise hearsay. But I must admit that her faith remained a mystery that needs to be solved. Sometimes I did not doubt that she was a true believer; at other times I could not fathom her. Did she feign piousness to strengthen her position as queen? Did she mean to encourage her husband to become more immersed in religion so that she could become the sole ruler of the land and the subjects? Was she merely a tool in her father's hand for some mysterious scheme? The priests tried to warn her, but she did not respond to them, with the result that their concern turned to spite. They were convinced that Akhenaten was weak, and they could not imagine that he was capable of challenging them. Because of that, they accused Tiye of being the source of his ideas, and blamed his stubbornness and persistence on Nefertiti. That, I believe, is nonsense. They can point their fingers at whoever they want, but I have no doubt that this foolishness was the product of Akhenaten's own mind. By moving to the new capital, Akhenaten declared war on all the deities.

He became a missionary, preaching his religion throughout the provinces. We so much enjoyed the blissful days of victory and peace that I imagined that this young, feeble king was capable of demolishing the structure of life as we had always known it, and building it anew according to his designs. I followed in awe his eloquent conquests of the provinces and the frenzy with which the people received him. I felt that a new kind of power had possessed him and that he excelled in exercising it. But at the back of my mind there was always a hint of doubt that this new world that was being created so quickly could last. Could order be achieved by the exercise of love alone? What were we supposed to make then of what we had experienced in the long life of our country? On one occasion Nefertiti said to me, as if she could read my thoughts, "He is inspired. God has blessed him with divine love. We shall be victorious and God will be by our side."

One time I sat alone with the minister Nakht, casually drinking wine. I believed, and I still do, that Nakht was a persuasive politician. I asked him, "Do you really believe in the One and Only, the god of love and peace?"

"Yes," he replied calmly, "but I don't support the seizure of other deities."

I was relieved. "A compromise then? Did you counsel the king?"

"Yes. He thought it heresy."

"And Nefertiti?"

"She speaks his tongue now," he said sorrowfully.

———

Then Haremhab told me how peace and happiness eventually turned to a promise of destruction. Again, he did not add to what the high priest or Ay had already told me.

———

At that point I tried to advise Akhenaten. "We must change our policy," I said. But he rejected every proposition I made that hinted of any compromise. The challenge seemed to inspire him even more.

"We must go ahead with our holy war until the very end," he said. "And there shall be no other end but victory."

Then he patted my shoulder gently and continued, "You must not share with the wretched ones their love of misery."

When the condition of the country continued to deteriorate I wished once more that I could kill him, this time out of love and loyalty. It became clear that what I thought was an incredible power in his feeble body was in reality a raging madness that must be curbed. The queen mother visited us when things were at their worst, and summoned me to her palace in the southern quarters of Akhetaten. "Perhaps you will succeed where we have failed," I said.

She stared at me intently, then asked, "I trust you have advised the pharaoh of the changes you thought necessary to rectify the situation."

I had heard how Tiye interpreted any hesitation preceding an answer, so I replied quickly, "I suggested, Your Majesty, a change in the country's home and foreign policies."

She seemed relieved. "This is what I expect from a loyal man like you, Haremhab."

"He is my king and my friend, as you now, Your Highness."

"Will you promise me, Haremhab, to remain loyal under any circumstances?" she asked, gazing straight into my eyes.

I thought quickly, and replied, "I promise you my loyalty regardless of the circumstances."

It was clear that she was relieved. "They are asking for his head. You have the power to keep him safe from harm. Sooner or later they will try to draw you to their side."

I repeated my promise to remain truthful and loyal to the king. Indeed I kept my promise; to abandon him in Akhetaten was the only way to protect him. Tiye failed to dissuade him, despite all her powers of persuasion. She left Akhetaten, to die with her fears. When the grip tightened on the city, I was certain beyond doubt that the new god was incapable of defending himself, let alone his beloved chosen king. We drank the bitterness of isolation, and death loomed over and around us. Yet the pharaoh did not waver; if anything, he seemed more determined. The flame of his spirit refused to die.

"My God will never let me down," he continued to say. Whenever I saw his face glowing with confidence, intoxicated, I became more certain that he was afflicted with insanity. It might have appeared a religious battle on the surface, but in truth it was sheer madness raging in the mind of a man born with a halo of perversity.

Then there was the visit of the high priest of Amun and his last warning to us. He grasped my hand firmly and said, "Haremhab, you are a man of many merits. Relieve your conscience of its burden and do what is expected of a man in your position."

To tell you the truth, I admired the man for rising above any desire to avenge himself, and for his attempt to spare the country more woes. We asked to meet with the king. It was a difficult, painful, sad meeting. It was as if we were shrugging off our loyalty to a man who knew nothing but love, a man who created a wonderful dream from the sparks of madness and wanted nothing more than to share it with us. I advised him to decree freedom of worship and initiate an immediate plan to defend the empire from the attacks of the enemies on the border. When he refused I suggested that he relinquish his obligations as pharaoh and devote his time to his religious calling. We gave him time to consider our counsel. Then he appointed Smenkhkare a co-ruler on the throne, and although Nefertiti left him, he still persisted. We therefore decided to abandon him and make peace with his enemies to preserve the unity of the country. We made this decision only after agreeing that no one should harm him or his wife. I gave the oath before the new king, Tutankhamun. That was the last episode in the greatest tragedy in Egypt's history. You see what madness has done to our country?

————

Haremhab and I embraced the silence that usually accompanies endings. I began to gather my papers to get ready to leave. Then it occurred to me to ask, "Why do you think she left him? Nefertiti I mean."

He replied without hesitation. "She must have realized that his madness was now jeopardizing her own life, so she left his palace to save herself."

"But why would she stay in the city? Why not leave Akhetaten with the rest of you?"

He replied scornfully. "She was sure the priests considered her equally culpable in her husband's crimes."

As I shook his hand to bid him farewell, I said, "How did he die?"

"His natural weakness made him incapable of bearing the defeat. His faith was shaken when his god forsook him. He fell ill for a few days, and died."

"How did you receive the news of his death, Commander?" I asked after some hesitation.

"I have said all I have to say," he replied stonily.

Bek

———

I met Bek, the sculptor, in his house on one of the islands of the Nile two miles south of Thebes. He lived in virtual isolation in a small but elegant house in the center of his modest farm. Bek was widely known to have excelled in his vocation above any other sculptor, but when our country was being rebuilt after the wars he was not summoned to participate as were many others of his standing. Bek was known for his loyalty to his former king, Akhenaten. In fact he was occasionally accused of being a heretic himself. Now he was almost forty years old, a strong, dark man, tall, slender, and full of energy. But his gaze was overcast by melancholy. He greeted me with a warm smile as he opened the letter that my father had given me. When he finished reading, he began.

———

Beauty and peace vanished when Akhenaten left our world, and I no longer find pleasure in color or in music.

I first knew him when I was still a young boy learning the basics of my vocation at the school of my father, Menn, the sculptor of King Amenhotep III. One day a young boy, carried on a sedan chair, visited us at school. My father whispered to me, "The crown prince."

I saw a lad of my own age, then, frail, unassuming, but with a piercing look. He seemed fascinated by the mere encounter of the chisel and the rock, as though it were a miracle. He came to watch and learn, and he engaged us in conversation with such friendliness that we soon forgot he was a member of the pharaoh's family. He continued to visit the school regularly, and we became friends. I was extremely happy with our friendship. My father took pride in our acquaintance and granted us his blessing.

"Akhenaten is a young boy with the wisdom of a man, my son," my father would say.

Indeed he was. Even the high priest of Amun acknowledged his wisdom and his maturity at such an early age. The priests interpreted it as an evil force that had taken hold of Akhenaten. That was not true, Meriamun. The evil force dwelt in the hearts of the priests. My king knew no evil. Perhaps that was his tragedy. Once, when we were young men, my father was absorbed in carving a sculpture for King Amenhotep III, and Akhenaten was watching him as he worked with his assistants.

"Master Menn," Akhenaten said, "you insist on all these traditional methods. I find them stifling."

"Tradition is power, Your Highness. With tradition

we can overcome the passage of time," my father answered with pride.

"Every sunrise brings a new kind of beauty," Akhenaten said ecstatically. Then he turned to me. "Bek, my friend, this sculpture may be beautiful but it will not be truthful. Where is the truth?"

Akhenaten lived for the truth, and because of the truth he died. From a very young age his soul was inspired with all that was mystical, as though he had been born from the womb of spirituality. He said to me once, "I am very fond of you, Bek. If you master your art I will entrust to you all matters of art and aesthetics when I become king."

The truth is that I owe Akhenaten everything, religion and art together. First he taught me the religion of Aten, then he showed me the path of the One God. I was filled with peace when I heard him recite with faith and love:

The land is bright with thy light
And is no more in darkness,
O Lord,
Master of the universe,
Of heaven and earth,
Of man and animal,
O our Creator.

One day, as we were walking from the quarry to school, I said, "My Prince, I believe in your God."

He was overjoyed. "You are the second believer after Meri-Ra; but our enemies will be plentiful."

I learned later that Nefertiti had joined the faith at the same time, while she was still at her father's palace. Akhenaten used to talk to me occasionally about the difficulties he faced because of his religion. Despite my isolation in the quarry, I was able to acquire some understanding of the events that transpired.

It was from my father that I learned the fundamentals of my vocation, but Akhenaten gave me the spirit. He committed himself to the truth, both in life and in art. Because of that he provoked those who lived only for this transient life, those who swarmed around every banquet like vultures and crows.

"Bek," he told me once, "do not let the teachings of the dead shackle your hands when you work. Let your stone be a harbor for truth. It is God who created everything, so be loyal to him in your representations. Do not allow fear or greed to influence your work. When you make a sculpture of me, let it show every flaw on my face and body so that the beauty of your work will be in its honesty."

That was Akhenaten, who rejected the old ways and was fascinated by novelty.

He renounced the idols and pulled out timeworn tradition by the root. Akhenaten found ecstasy in truth.

When he became king, I declared my faith again before him and he appointed me first sculptor of the king. When God inspired him to build the new city and move his throne to it, I was in charge of eighty thousand workers, building the most beautiful city ever known, the city of light and faith, Akhetaten.

We built the largest roads, the finest palaces, and the most beautiful of gardens and ponds. It was an artist's masterpiece, but in the end it fell prey to the malice of the priests.

———

Bek remained silent for a while, unable to conceal his grief for his most cherished creation, which was now slowly vanishing into the dust of the earth. I, too, remained silent out of respect for him, until finally he continued.

———

Akhenaten was an artist himself. He recited poetry, painted, and even tried his slender hand at carving stone. I will tell you a secret that few people know. He carved a sculpture of Nefertiti that was by all standards an ideal of beauty. It may still be in the abandoned palace, or in Nefertiti's palace, or perhaps it was destroyed with everything else. When the queen abandoned him unexpectedly, he took out the left eye of the sculpture to express his disappointment, but left the rest of it intact as a token of eternal love.

The queen and Akhenaten were a symbol of the God who was father and mother in one. They were united by a deep love that weathered many storms. I still do not understand why she left him at the very end. Her enemies accused her of leaving the sinking ship. They said she wanted to find herself a place in the new nation. But she did not try to win anyone over after that. Of her own will, she remained isolated in her palace, until it became her prison. It was not true that she had been nursing her own interest. I believe that her faith might have been shaken when God did not come to their aid at the time of those painful events. In a dark hour she deserted both the throne and her religion. As for Akhenaten, he was determined until the end. How could he give up his faith when it was he who had heard the heavenly voice of God call him his dear son? After that Akhenaten could not hear any other voice, nor did he care for any other opinion or listen to anyone's advice as a person should when he seeks the truth. It was not he who was defeated, but us. I, too, had my doubts, particularly when they asked him to relinquish the throne, and even more when everyone abandoned him. I saw him once standing alone, calmly watching everyone leave. When he saw me approach he said, "You must go with them, Bek."

"No one dared speak to me of this, my King," I said agitatedly.

"But you will go," he replied with a smile.

"I will remain by my king forever."

"Bek," he said gently, "you will go, whether willingly, or by force."

I remained silent for a moment, then asked, "My Master, can evil overcome?"

He seemed to disappear in his thoughts for a moment, then I heard him say, "Evil can never overcome. What we are witnessing is only a fleeting moment. Only death can keep us from seeing the truth."

Then he began to sing:

You dwell within me, My Lord.
No other has known you
But your son Akhenaten.
You inspire me with your knowledge.
You are the power of creation.

———

In the same way that he never gave up his faith, he never stopped loving either. Even when he saw the pyramid he built destroyed, and saw his own men join his enemies and his beloved wife desert him without explanation, even then his heart did not know a moment of hatred or spite. He was above punishment; he had nothing but love for man, animal, and even inanimate matter. When he first took the throne, Egypt was a vast empire with loving, obedient subjects. He could have chosen to indulge in worldly comforts: women, wine, food. But he looked away from such temptations and gave himself to the truth, challenging the powers of greed and selfishness. So he sacrificed everything, without ever losing the smile on his face.

"Why don't you use force to defend love and peace?" I asked him one day after the seeds of evil had started growing.

He replied, "Vicious people and criminals always find an excuse to justify their thirst for blood, and I am not one of those, Bek."

I will never forget his kindness when he sensed that I

liked Mutnedjmet, his sister-in-law. He tried to pave the way for me to ask her hand in marriage. When she refused me he consoled me: "Do not be sorry, she is like a vulture waiting for her chance to attack." I asked him what he meant, but he did not answer.

When everyone else had left, I insisted on remaining with him, as did Meri-Ra, the priest of the One God. But the sage Ay met with us and said, "We are only leaving to protect him from an attack that we cannot ward off. It is the only way we can save his life. Believe me, if anyone was to remain with him I would have chosen to be that one. I am the father of his wife, and his first teacher."

"But Ay, my staying with him will not change the course of events anyhow."

"The agreement between us and the priests was that Akhenaten would not be harmed, on the condition that none of his followers and men remain in the city with him. The priests will assign a few servants to watch over him."

My heart was seared with pain as I was forced to join everyone else. I still have doubts, for I, too, cannot understand why God abandoned him. Sometimes I pray to God and sometimes not. When I received the news of his death, I wept until my eyes exhausted their tears. I had a deep feeling that he did not just die but that they killed him by sorcery or in some other brutal way. Now, here I am living without purpose or a trace of happiness, waiting for death to take me, as it took my beautiful city.

T a d u k h i p a

Tadukhipa was the daughter of Tushratta, the king of Mitanni, Egypt's closest ally. At the end of his life, King Amenhotep III married Tadukhipa. He was sixty years old and she was fifteen. When Amenhotep died and Akhenaten became king, he inherited Tadukhipa as a part of his father's harem. Now she lives in a palace in northern Thebes with three hundred slaves in her service. She agreed to speak to me only on the recommendation of Haremhab. She was a beautiful woman, in her thirties, with an aura of mystery and dignity. I met her in the grand reception room, where she was seated on a chair of ebony inlaid with gold. Her smile encouraged me to ask her to tell her story.

I lived with King Amenhotep III for a very short period, a period filled with jealousy and bitterness. When I met the Great Queen Tiye I was rather surprised. I could not understand how a woman like her was able to rise to such status. In my father's palace the likes of Tiye were more than happy just to serve in his harem. I was even more surprised when I first saw the crown prince walking in the garden. What a wasted and hideous creature he was. I felt more contempt than pity for him.

Soon after my marriage to Amenhotep III his health began to deteriorate. Some spiteful people dared to blame me for the king's ill health. My concerns, however, were different. From the very first night of our marriage I could see in the king's wrinkled face my imminent misfortune—that wretched boy would soon take me as part of his inheritance. I found myself thinking that life with his old father was probably better than life with him. After all, Amenhotep III, despite what one might expect of an ailing man his age, was lively, cheerful, and full of vigor. In the harem quarters the woman often talked about the crown prince. We amused ourselves by making fun of his passion for feminine art forms like painting and singing, and his dubious disinterest in women. We thought he was quite unfit for the throne.

Soon the news arrived about his obsession with a new religion, and the trouble this was causing his parents. We heard that the priests of Amun were alarmed. We were curious about all this but, really, it had very little effect on us; in the harem, the daily concerns of women came before those of the country. It was only the king's death that shook us and threw us into a quandary we did not know how to escape. The loathsome creature was crowned king and shared the throne with Nefertiti, whom he had married when his father was still alive. And, yes, we all became his possession. It is true that he was very generous in the care he provided us, but he kept us like tamed animals without once coming near any of us. As a result of his neglect, the women soon engaged in perverse relations to gratify their desires.

"Why doesn't he pay attention to us instead of these religious feuds with the priests and everyone else?" one of the women asked.

"He must be impotent; why else would he bother with all that religious nonsense?" another replied.

Nevertheless, Nefertiti was very jealous, and decided to pay a visit to the harem. The women rightly guessed her real motive. Nefertiti wanted to see me, because she had heard in the palace that I was young and beautiful. I was the only one in the harem who was close to her in age and just as beautiful. Indeed I was of rather better descent. I was the daughter of a king, while her father Ay was just a commoner. Ay was one of the first to declare his faith in the new religion. Later, when Akhenaten's sun was setting, he was the first to abandon him and join his enemies. In any event, the new queen came to the harem surrounded by slave girls. She greeted us, one woman after the other in order of seniority. When it was my turn—and I was the last—she looked at me with piercing eyes, full of curiosity. I stood before her defiantly until her face grew somber. I was not surprised to hear that she was furious at the queen mother for advising her son to pay attention to his duties toward his harem, and especially to me, the daughter of Tushratta, Egypt's friend and ally. Indeed Nefertiti did not forgive

Tiye for pressuring Akhenaten in this way. She became even more enraged when the king yielded to his mother's will and decided to pay me a visit.

I waited for Akhenaten, as instructed, in my room on my gold-inlaid bed, completely naked, in all my beauty. He arrived wearing only a short loincloth, and sat on the edge of the bed, smiling softly.

"Would it make you happy to bear me a child?" he whispered.

I tried to ignore the feeling of disgust that came over me. "It is my duty, your Highness."

"But it is love I am after." There was a look of desperation in his eyes. "Love is my only duty."

"Is it love that inspires your desire for me, Master?"

"Forgive me." He stroked the back of my hand tenderly, kissed me on the forehead, then left the room as calmly as he had entered.

I did not tell anyone what happened in my room that night, and most of the women in the harem thought that Nefertiti had lost at least half the king's heart. Days passed and we continued to receive news of events outside the palace. Then we heard about the king's decision to build a new city, and in a matter of a few years we moved to Akhetaten. In the new city, everyone was happy but us. We were cast off in a remote quarter of the palace, where we lived an unbearable and utterly degrading life that bred further perversity. When it became known that the idiot king wanted to fight sin with love instead of punishment, those in the harem who had not resorted to sleeping with other women had no qualms about inviting the palace guards to their beds. The moral system fell apart. Nevertheless, the king's only concern was to spread his new religion in the provinces. All the women around me began to pray to the One and Only God, without true belief. Akhenaten's religion, I thought then, was the only religion without believers. I still think that his religion created a nation of hypocrites and people greedy for power and wealth. I just could not fathom how this vast universe could have only one god. Why, every city needs a god to look after its affairs; every human activity requires a god that knows about it. Besides, how could people relate to each other with love only? What nonsense! His mother must have spoilt him completely, for him to be so irrational. He often recited poetry in front of large audiences, and then his wife would sing. The sacred throne was overtaken by a mob of rascal poets and singers and the dignity of the pharaohs was shattered.

What followed was inevitable. Misery was everywhere, like a long night promising no dawn. Disasters hailed on the country and the whole empire. My father was one of the few allies who remained loyal to Egypt during those frightful times, until finally he was killed in battle, defending an idiot king. Some people thought the problem was that Akhenaten was a noble poet misplaced on the throne by a twist of fate. But the truth is that he was a strange creature, neither man nor woman, driven by shame and stigma to destroy himself and the country. He wanted to hold up love as a beacon for everyone; instead enmity and malice spread like fire in people's hearts and his empire was extinguished. As for his cunning wife, Nefertiti, she only went along with this nonsense in the hope of having exclusive access to authority, and to gratify her insatiable lust with as many men as she desired. Nefertiti managed to convince everyone that she and her husband were a model of love and fidelity. They would actually kiss before their subjects on the streets of Akhetaten and at provincial conventions. But it was a well-known fact among the women in the palace that the king and his wife never slept together. Akhenaten was incapable of such things with women. Nefertiti had relationships with the sculptor Bek, the general Haremhab, Mae, and many others—which is how she got her six daughters. There were rumors among the slave girls that the only sexual relation Akhenaten ever had was with his mother, Queen Tiye.

Tadukhipa must have noticed my confusion for she observed me silently for some time. Then she continued.

It was known in the harem that Tiye bore him a daughter. That was an unquestionable fact. More than one slave girl testified that she had seen Akhenaten and Tiye having sex. Certainly it was no secret to Nefertiti, which was why the two women despised each other.

The problem was that most people could not imagine how this man who caused so much tumult in the world was in essence such a worthless, despicable being.

That, however, is the truth that must be known and recorded in history. If Akhenaten had not been born in one of the greatest families in history he would have lived a low life in the alleys of Thebes, slavering like a madman, an object of children's mockery. No wonder then that the empire collapsed during his reign. As for Nefertiti, if it had not been for Akhenaten, she would have been a professional whore.

A short while before the tragedy ended, the queen mother came to Akhetaten hoping to save the ship from sinking. There was a fierce argument between Tiye and Nefertiti. Nefertiti accused Tiye of collaborating with the enemies of the throne.

Akhenaten was deeply pained by his wife's accusation and defended his mother—or his lover I should say—vehemently.

That, of course, angered Nefertiti, but she kept it to herself and then took her revenge by leaving him at the critical moment, with no explanation whatsoever.

Then she tried to gain the friendship of the priests to secure herself a place in the new era. Perhaps she even aspired to be the wife of Tutankhamun. But all her attempts were futile and if it had not been for the sway of her lover, Haremhab, the priests would have ripped her to pieces.

———

Tadukhipa was silent for a moment. Then she concluded, with a scornful smile, "This is the story of the imbecile king, Akhenaten, and his absurd religion."

d bluox

Toto

———

"I never renounced Amun, nor did I join the caravan of hypocrites and opportunists. I served the heretic in agreement with the high priest of Amun. I was the watchful eye that protected Amun, and the first that struck in his defense."

Thus began Toto, the chief epistoler in Akhenaten's chamber. Clearly it agonized him to think that he, too, like all the others who served Akhenaten, would be regarded as a hypocrite. I met him in his vestry in the temple, where he resumed his work as chanter priest in the Tutankhamun era, the position he had had when Amenhotep III was pharaoh. He had a fleshy face with bulging eyes, but his outstanding feature was his ill temper. He was eager to tell me his version of the tragedy.

———

The heretic's forefathers were great kings. Trouble started when Amenhotep III chose a partner on the throne from the common people and she bore him that stupid, mad son, the crown prince. Amenhotep III and Queen Tiye had adopted a new policy toward the priests of Amun. They appreciated the merit and status of Amun and believed in him as master of all deities. At the same time they paid enough attention to the priests of other gods, so as to secure the loyalty of everyone. Together, the priests of other deities were an equal power to the priests of Amun. Thus the throne used the priests to curb each other, and the king and queen monopolized power in the country. We were not particularly fond of this policy, yet we had enough privileges that we were not offended, and we did not protest. After all, Amun was the holiest of all deities as far as the people were concerned.

When Akhenaten became king, the path was clear before him. He could have taken the same course as his forefathers and walked it peacefully. But the mouse fancied himself a lion. Therein was the catastrophe. He lacked the wisdom and power of his predecessors. He was haunted by his natural weakness, his ugliness, and his womanliness. Such malice and deception can only come of weakness and jealousy. Thus he decided to get rid of all the priests in the country and claim sole power for himself.

He declared himself the only god with no partner but an illusory god that he used as a mask for his ambition. In the beginning we heard news about the miracles of the young lad who had matured beyond his tender years. Then came the story of the new god who revealed himself to him and asked him to renounce all other deities. That day I said to the high priest, "It is a conspiracy that must be killed in its cradle." He did not seem convinced. I continued, "I suspect that Queen Tiye and the sage Ay are behind all this. The boy is merely a tool."

The high priest said, "The queen is partly responsible, no doubt. But her mistake is one of bad judgment. That is what I hold against her, not a conspiracy. As for Ay, I think he is no less alarmed than we are."

I believed him, for the high priest is infallible. "Then the boy must be possessed by the spirit of Set, god of evil. He must be slain immediately."

"Have patience, Toto," the high priest said. "I believe it is not beyond the king and queen to put things right."

I was convinced that our hesitation would prove to be very costly. I prayed to Amun:

Amun,
Master of the silent ones,
Father of the poor,
When I call upon you
You heed my pleas,
O Amun, Master of Thebes,
Savior from the nether world.

————

Toto continued with events I had heard about before— the crown prince's tour of the empire, his return, and his succession as pharaoh of Egypt.

Men declared their faith in exchange for high-ranking positions. They dropped their dignity and swarmed like flies around the heretic. In time his venom poisoned the entire country. Treason. That is what it was, treason beyond any justification. They are all responsible for the destruction that came upon us.

"There is no crime without punishment," I said to the high priest. "We must take Akhetaten and kill them all; the heretic and his wife, Ay, Haremhab, Nakht, and Bek."

"The country cannot bear any more destruction," the high priest replied.

"Only blood will quench the thirst of Amun," I insisted.

"I believe I know more of what would satisfy Amun."

I said no more, but the flames of rage continued to burn inside me. I believe that the absence of punishment encourages crime and breeds evil among people. They begin to question divine justice. It pains me to see people without honor enjoy the peace and comfort that belongs to those who do have honor. Why should we protect those who contributed to our own destruction?

Toto went on to tell me about the building of Akhetaten, the exodus to the new city, and Akhenaten's rising fervor in spreading his religion through the country.

In Akhetaten I worked in the heretic's chamber. As I heard more of his ravings I realized the extent of his madness. He should have been a poet or a singer. Instead he was king of Egypt. Catastrophe! He concealed his weakness behind a veil of mystical inspiration. Some believed him, and others decided it was sheer madness. It was neither piousness nor hallucination; it was the shrewdness of a man humiliated by his own weakness, a man with no other power than deception. It was by deception that he monopolized the rule of Egypt. He had an aching desire to prove that even without military conquests and physical strength, he was still more powerful than Tuthmosis III. He created a fantasy world, with ludicrous laws and customs; even the people in it were his own fabrication. Akhenaten was master and god of an illusion. It is no wonder then that his kingdom tumbled down with the first winds of reality, and the mob of cowards he had gathered fled at the first sign of danger.

People marveled every time the heretic went into a trance. They talked endlessly about the remarkable, unearthly words that flowed from him like a stream of magical melody. I witnessed some of these trances myself. As I reviewed the epistles before him, he would suddenly yield to a gush of intense sentiment, gradually withdrawing from the bounds of awareness to fade into the unknown. Eventually he returned to his senses. "God will persevere," he would say. At those times I would steal glances at Haremhab, Ay, and Nakht, and wonder if they really believed him. As for me, I thought it was an obscene mockery of everything we held sacred. And in truth, none of them believed him either. Their faith in his god was a means to an end. Ultimately, they abandoned him, and so demonstrated that their only loyalty was to their inexhaustible ambition.

————

Toto told me about the corruption of the civil servants, the suffering of the citizens, the spread of rebellion, the attacks on the borders of the empire, and the tragic death of Egypt's most powerful ally, Tushratta, king of Mitanni.

"I was consumed with fear for the future of Egypt," he continued. "I made a plan to have him killed, to save the world his evil. It was easy enough to find someone eager to do it. I arranged a hiding place for him in the palace garden where the king retired to be alone. The man would have succeeded in his mission if it was not for Maho, chief of guards, who saw him at the last minute. By killing him Maho earned the eternal curse of the deities. Finally, I resorted to sorcery. That failed, too; most likely it could not withstand the counter-spells of the heretic and his men."

————

Toto then told me about the visit of Queen Tiye to Akhetaten, and the extraordinary meeting between the priest of Amun and the men of Akhenaten.

————

When the king learned that the priests were claiming the throne for Tutankhamun, thus pressuring him to abdicate, he declared his brother Smenkhkare co-regent. But his entire world fell apart when Nefertiti left the palace. That was the end of evil; only by that time the serpent had injected its venom. Akhenaten's union with Nefertiti was a grave misfortune for Egypt. Nefertiti was undeniably a strong, capable, and wise queen. And a very beautiful one indeed. But, like her husband, ambition plagued her. She claimed that she shared Akhenaten's faith in the One God. In reality she only shared with him his wickedness and deception. She never loved him. She could not have loved him even if she wanted to. Her single true passion was for absolute power. Perhaps Nefertiti was a final proof of the role Ay played in the tragedy; she was the product of her father's flaws. I remember how Ay and his wife sat grandly on the terrace of the palace during public ceremonies, receiving gifts of pure gold. At the end of the ceremony, slaves carried large baskets filled with these gifts to the sage's palace. It is hard to imagine, nevertheless, how a seemingly reasonable woman like Nefertiti would be so blind to the grave repercussions of her husband's policies. Did she really believe in the god of love and joy? I find that hard to swallow. I believe Nefertiti made an error in overestimating the influence of the throne on the people of Egypt. She was under the illusion that she could use the throne like a magician's wand to justify the most appalling deeds. Perhaps she realized her mistake early on but was reluctant to voice her concerns for fear of losing her husband's trust. When the men decided to leave Akhetaten, Nefertiti abandoned the king, desperately hoping that her lovers would not betray her. I believe Haremhab tried to convince the high priest of Amun to allow her to return to Thebes, but his efforts were to no avail. Eventually the heretic died. Nefertiti still lives in her prison, bitter and regretful.

Had Egypt's fiercest enemy seized the throne after Amenhotep III, he could not have done as much damage as that accursed heretic.

Tey

———

Tey was the wife of the sage Ay. She was seventy years old, a woman of small stature but strong and charming. She had married Ay after the death of his first wife. Nefertiti was a child of one or two years at most when Tey married her father. Not too long after, Tey gave birth to Mutnedjmet. Tey was not a typical stepmother; she was extremely fond of Nefertiti. Likewise, when Nefertiti became queen, she chose Tey as one of her maids of honor and gave her the title of queen's matron.

I related to Tey the information I had obtained thus far. "I do not wish to encroach on your time. If you have nothing to add I shall leave you in peace." But Tey began to tell her story.

———

I did not know the king all that well, despite the intimacy I shared with his wife. Indeed he addressed me personally only a few times. But his sweetness has never left me. My husband had been his tutor since he was a boy, so we got to hear a lot about him. Mutnedjmet and I were quite disturbed by his offensive opinions about Amun, his attraction to Aten, and finally his claim to have found a new god. Nefertiti, however, did not share our concerns.

I ought to tell you a few things about Nefertiti first. She was a very intelligent young woman, eager and passionate, inspired by beauty, and intensely drawn to the mystical questions of religion. She seemed so mature for her age that one day I said to Ay, "It seems that your daughter will become a priestess!"

Nefertiti and Mutnedjmet used to bicker sometimes, the way sisters do, but Nefertiti was always in the right. I do not recall a single time when I could place the blame on her. And she always made up with her sister, as an elder sister should do. As for her education, she was so very good that I was afraid my daughter might do something dreadful out of jealousy.

The first thing we noticed was that she would listen admiringly as her father told us about the crown prince. Then she seemed to be developing an immense liking for Aten. But when she broke the news that she now believed in Akhenaten's One and Only God, we were aghast. "But Akhenaten is a heretic," Mutnedjmet said to Nefertiti.

"He has heard the voice of God," Nefertiti replied confidently.

"Then you, too, are a heretic," Mutnedjmet cried.

Nefertiti had a very beautiful voice, and we used to enjoy hearing her sing:

What should I say to Mother?
Every day I brought back game.
This time I set not the snares,
For by your love I was possessed.

After she declared her new faith, we often heard her singing alone in the garden to her new god, but then we showed no enthusiasm, not even for her heavenly voice. We did not want to encourage her. I still remember clearly hearing her as I stood in my room combing my hair one morning:

O Eternal One,
O Graceful and Mighty One,
In thee we rejoice
And the universe has filled
With light.

Our palace became one of the first places where the hymns of the new religion echoed. Then one day we were invited to celebrate the thirtieth anniversary of the coronation of Amenhotep III. We were allowed for the first time to extend the invitation to our daughters, so that they, too, could witness a celebration in the pharaonic palace. I was delighted at the idea that Nefertiti and Mutnedjmet might appeal to some of the eligible young men at the party, and I made sure they were dressed for the occasion. They wore beautiful flowing dresses, with embroidered shawls draped over their shoulders, and golden sandals with high straps.

When we arrived at the royal palace, we entered a hall the size of our entire house. Along the walls flaming torches encircled the guest seats. The throne was set up between two rows of seats for princes and princesses. The center of the room was left for the musicians and naked dancers. Slaves moved among the guests carrying censers and trays loaded with the most exquisite food and drink. I looked over the best of the young men in the hall. For my two daughters I fancied the aspiring officer Haremhab and the talented sculptor Bek. Then I saw how the eyes of the notables, Haremhab, Bek, Nakht, Mae, and many others, followed Nefertiti, particularly when the chance came for the young noblewomen to dance and sing before the king. My beloved Nefertiti danced so elegantly and sang with such a sweet, captivating voice that she outdid the professional singers. Perhaps for that one night I shared Mutnedjmet's silent jealousy. I found solace in thinking that if Nefertiti was married, Mutnedjmet's light could shine unrivaled. I watched Nefertiti curiously, to see if her attention was drawn to anyone in particular. I was surprised to see that she was looking toward her spiritual master, the crown prince. I glanced in his direction and was appalled by his strange appearance.

"I pictured him a giant," Nefertiti whispered to me when our eyes met.

Yet her fascination was greater than her surprise,

though I am certain she did not even dream what destiny had in store for her. When we returned to our palace I said to my husband, "The suitors will come knocking on our door, so be prepared."

"The gods chart our destiny," he replied in his usual calm voice.

When a day or two had passed, Ay delivered some surprising news to us. "The queen wishes to meet Nefertiti," he said.

We were taken aback. "What does this mean, Ay?" I asked.

He pondered for a while, then said, "She may want to offer her a position in the palace."

"But you must know more."

"How can I know what is in the Great Queen's mind, Tey?"

Ay taught Nefertiti the protocol for meeting Her Majesty. I asked Amun to bless and protect her.

"I ask the protection of the One and Only God," Nefertiti protested.

"Do not utter such foolishness in the presence of the queen," Ay scolded her.

When she returned after meeting the queen she was so overwhelmed by emotion that she threw her arms around me and burst into tears.

"The queen has chosen her to be the wife of the crown prince," Ay announced.

We were overjoyed. Nefertiti had risen above any jealousy we might have harbored in our hearts. She had opened the door for us to become part of the pharaoh's family, and her good fortune elevated us above the rest. I congratulated her from the depths of my heart, and so did Mutnedjmet. Nefertiti told us everything that had happened between her and the Great Queen, but I was so excited that I did not really listen properly. In fact, I do not recall any of what she said. But what is the importance of words compared to the event itself?

The marriage ceremony was so lavish that it reminded all the elders of the wedding of Amenhotep III. We became related to royalty, and my dear Nefertiti appointed me queen's matron, a position that ranked next to princess. In marriage Nefertiti and the prince became one soul that could be separated only by death. She shared his joy and his sorrow until just hours before the end. She managed with him the affairs of the country with the skill of a woman born to the throne. She shared with him the weight of his religious message as though she had been chosen by the One God to be his priestess. Believe me, she was a great queen in every way, so I was shocked at the news of her sudden desertion of her husband in extreme adversity. That was perhaps the only decision she made without consulting me. I hurried to her palace and sat at her feet, overcome by tears. She did not seem to be affected by my grief.

"Go in peace," she said calmly.

"Those who have abandoned the king are only complying to protect him from danger, but you . . . ," I pleaded.

"Go in peace," she interrupted me coldly.

"And you, Your Highness?" I asked in disbelief.

"I will not leave this palace," she replied.

I was about to say more but she stopped me with a firm voice. "Go in peace."

When I left her palace I was the most miserable woman in the universe. For a long time I tried to think what could have driven her to disappear and isolate herself in that way. Only one reason seemed feasible: Nefertiti had so dreaded seeing the king fall that she preferred, in a moment of desperation, to flee. Yet I am certain that she left with the intention of returning to him after all the others had gone, just as I am certain that she must have tried to return but was prevented by force. Do not believe anyone who says otherwise. You will hear conflicting accounts and every man will claim to have spoken the truth, but they all have their biases. Life has taught me not to trust or believe anyone. Here we are now, so much time has passed, and I still wonder: Did Akhenaten deserve such a sad end? He was a noble, truthful, compassionate man. Why did they not return his love, why did they attack him like animals, tearing him and his kingdom apart as if he was their enemy? I saw him in my dreams a few years ago. He was lying on the ground, blood seeping out of a deep wound in his neck. I'm sure they killed him and made out he had died a natural death.

Mutnedjmet

————

Mutnedjmet was in her early forties, beautiful, slim, her honey-colored eyes gleaming with intelligence. I felt in her presence a distance that could not be readily crossed. Mutnedjmet is the daughter of Ay and Tey, and sister of Nefertiti. She lives in a private suite in Ay's palace. She never married, though she had several suitors. Why this should be remains a great mystery. The moment I sat before her and spread my papers she began to talk.

————

It was destined that we take part in the tragedy of the heretic. My father Ay was chosen to be his teacher, and through him we heard about the prince's peculiar ideas. From the very beginning I did not think well of him. I doubted his sanity, and in time I was proven right. Nefertiti, on the other hand, took a different stand. I had always known that she had an insatiable craving for attention. She would often whip up storms from trivial arguments just to entertain herself. Yet I was still surprised when she declared her opinion on the ravings of the crown prince. There is no question that she had a brilliant, astute mind. But her most virulent flaw was that she was incapable of being sincere. Thus she renounced the worship of Amun and replaced him with Aten. Indeed, she renounced all the gods and declared her faith in a god that we had never heard of before.

"Father," I overheard her say one afternoon, "tell the crown prince that I believe in his God."

"Don't be foolish," Father cried. "You do not realize the gravity of what you are saying."

I was afraid that her heresy would bring a curse upon us. My faith in my gods was never shaken. Yes, I declared my faith in the new god, but only out of necessity. After all, I was related to the pharaoh's family. Besides, I thought that I could probably defend my gods more effectively from within than if I had been cast out. But you must understand that my faith never faltered. Never.

I saw the heretic for the first time on the thirtieth anniversary of King Amenhotep III's rule. His physical appearance was as distorted as his ideas. Hideous and sickly, that was how I found him from the beginning. Don't believe what you heard about Akhenaten and Nefertiti's noble love. Nefertiti and I were raised together. I knew her too well to believe that that repulsive, effeminate creature had anything in common with the man of her dreams, whom she had longed for since we were young girls in our father's palace.

During the Sed festival, Nefertiti's true nature came out—a trained whore, exposing her beauty without shame. I remember she tried to get the attention of Haremhab, but he rejected her banality. When I was invited to perform before the king and queen, I danced with the dignity of a decent young woman from a noble family. Then I chose a song praising our great pharaoh:

In a festival of glory
You have come,
Like a bright horizon after a storm,
A refuge, an end to hunger.
You are a bringer of warmth.

As for Nefertiti, she appalled the audience with an obscene dance; of course she won the admiration of some vile spectators. To make matters worse, she sang like a born and bred whore:

Let us drink to your beauty
Until we are exhilarated.
Tonight I came to set the trap.
May we both be captured,
You and I, with no other.
Hold my hand, come,
We shall soon be there.

My father's head dropped in shame, and my mother stuttered before the censuring eyes that demanded an explanation. Even the professional entertainers whispered to each other in disbelief. That night, when we returned to our palace, I was certain that Haremhab was the subject of Nefertiti's dreams. She hoped that in the morning he would come knocking on her door. But destiny had yet to treat us, and indeed all of Egypt, to a momentous surprise. Nefertiti was invited to meet Queen Tiye. When she returned from the palace, she was Akhenaten's betrothed.

"Shouldn't the crown prince strengthen the succession of the throne by marrying a princess with royal blood?" I asked my mother.

"If the pharaoh has accepted the prince's intended bride knowing that she is not royalty, then it can't be important," Mother replied. "Remember, the pharaoh himself didn't marry a princess." Then she kissed my forehead tenderly and whispered, "Be patient, Mutnedjmet. There is no question that you are superior to Nefertiti in every way. But when fate is in command, we become helpless spectators. Try to be content with your lot. After all you will be the queen's sister, nothing short of a princess. You must not forget that your fortune will come to you inasmuch as you are loyal to your sister."

"Thank you for the advice, Mother," I replied firmly, "but I have enough wisdom to realize my new obligations. My loyalties, however, will not change."

Later, Nefertiti and I talked privately. "Are you really fond of him?" I asked.

"And who might you be referring to?" she teased.

"Your future husband, of course."

"He is a miracle among men," she replied enthusiastically.

"As a man, too?"

"There is no separation between the man in the priest and the priest in the man."

I knew what she was thinking; I could always read her mind. She would share the king's throne as queen and priestess, and gratify her lust elsewhere. And she carried through her decision, encouraged by her husband's impotency and his policy that abolished punishment. I learned about Akhenaten's perverse sexuality through my daily visits to the harem. There they knew facts that remained hidden from the closest of his men. It was the women of the harem who exposed the sinful relationship between the king and his mother, the only woman in whose embrace he was able to overcome his impotency. The Great Queen was both his mother and the mother of his daughter. Our country had never known such evil before. I knew then that I was destined to witness the darkest time in the history of Egypt. I vowed that I would always stand with the truth wherever it may be.

Amenhotep III died and Nefertiti became queen of Egypt and the empire. We lived some dreary days in Thebes, before moving to Akhetaten, the most beautiful city the world has known. It was magnificent in Akhetaten at first. Our days were full of joy and comfort. The gods gave the heretic a respite and paved the way for his success, but only so that he could indulge further in sin. Hence Amun was able to avenge himself just at the moment when Akhenaten thought that his god was victorious.

"Where are the gods?" I asked my mother in a moment of privacy. "Why don't they do something?"

"Mutnedjmet, this is a sign that the new god is the true one," she replied, much to my surprise.

I stared at her in disbelief. I felt as though the world I knew had come to an end, and that a new one was replacing it. But fast as it had come, the sweet dream Akhenaten had created began to fade, and the clouds of gloom rumbled on the distant horizon. In time, the grip grew tighter on Akhetaten.

"This is Amun venting his anger at last," I said to my father.

"You sound like those malicious priests."

"Tell me, Father, what really is your duty in a time like this?"

"I don't need to be reminded of my duty, Mutnedjmet," he replied irritably.

I asked Nefertiti once, "Will you not do something to defend your throne?"

"We do our best to serve the throne of the One God," she replied. I was not convinced by her enthusiasm.

You must not think that she spoke out of devotion. When it came to loyalty, Nefertiti was utterly lacking. She was merely afraid that if she warned her husband of the consequences of his stubbornness he would withdraw his trust from her and choose another woman to share his throne. During my attempts to talk some sense into Akhenaten's men, I discovered that Toto, the chief epistoler, had secretly harbored a loyalty to Amun. Toto became the middle man between me and the high priest of Amun. It was absolute torment. I had to choose between my family and my country and gods. By joining the priests' camp I risked the peace in my family, and even my own safety.

"The high priest wishes to win the queen to our side," Toto said one day. "He asked for your help."

"I have tried, believe me. You don't suppose I waited for the high priest to tell me something so obvious. Nefertiti, I admit, is no less foolish than the heretic."

The high priest convinced Queen Tiye to visit Akhetaten. When her attempts were to no avail, he came in person to deliver his last warning to Akhenaten's men. Toto did not agree with the high priest. He favored an unannounced raid upon them. "Set the heathen city on fire," he declared.

I so much wanted to win Haremhab, chief of security, to our side. He had insuperable power in Akhetaten. Since he had a reputation for being utterly candid, I was quite direct with him. I found, however, that he was very cautious. Perhaps he did not trust me, just as I did not fully trust him at first. Indeed, I had to discuss things with him several times before I became confident that he was in agreement with us. I waited until civil war loomed over Egypt.

"We must reassess our strategies," I said. Haremhab looked at me curiously, and I continued, "We cannot let Egypt burn to ashes."

"Did you not speak to your sister?" he asked cunningly.

"She speaks the king's tongue. They are both insane." My frankness startled him.

"What do you advise?" He appeared keen.

"Anything is permissible if it will save the country," I replied.

―――――

Mutnedjmet continued after a moment of silence. "It was truly a tragedy, even greater than the invasion of Egypt by the Hyksos. You must have heard several times how it all ended. Akhenaten was insane; unfortunately for all of us, he inherited the throne of Egypt and used it to exercise his morbid impulses. I place more blame on Nefertiti, for she is not lacking in reason. But she wanted only to nurse her ambition and cultivate more power. When Akhenaten's glory began to fade, she abandoned him just like that. She even tried to join his enemies; perhaps she hoped to be queen of the new throne. Look at her now, buried in dark solitude, bitter and full of regret."

Meri-Ra

———

Meri-Ra's face was a prelude to the sadness inside him. His skin was bronzed by the sun. He was slim, rather tall, in his mid-forties. He lived alone in a small house, with no companions or servant. Meri-Ra was once the high priest of the One and Only God in Akhetaten, the city of light. I visited him in his town, Deshasha, two days north of Thebes. When he read my father's letter he asked me, smiling, "Why do you take such a burden upon yourself?"

"To find out the truth," I answered.

"It is good to think that there is one person who seeks the truth," he nodded. "Perhaps I was the only one who was driven out of Akhetaten by force. I refused to abandon my king. The voice of God was silenced, the temple was destroyed, but destiny has yet to have its final word." Then he gazed at me with his sad brown eyes and began his story.

I was fortunate to have been among the prince's closest companions from boyhood. Akhenaten and I were greatly drawn to mystical themes. We studied the religion of Amun together, as well as Aten. Like many of our peers, I was enchanted with his charm. I admired his sensitivity and insight. He was a remarkable theologian. He blessed me with the words that later conquered everyone's heart: "I love you, Meri-Ra. Do not withhold your love from me."

His love penetrated my heart and spread to my soul. He often invited me to join him in his place of retreat on the western side of the palace by the Nile bank, an awning supported on four columns and surrounded by lotus and palm trees. Its floor was lush grass, and in the middle there was a green mat and a cushion. Akhenaten would wake up in the darkness of the early morning hours. When the golden sun emerged behind the fields, he sang to Aten. His sweet voice still echoes in my ears, and intoxicates me like the smell of holy incense:

> *Your light, a summit in the sky,*
> *Aten, the living God,*
> *Aten, the first of life,*
> *When your rays appear in the East*
> *The world is a festival of light.*
> *Aten, the living Sun,*
> *Aten, shining above,*
> *Your light unifies the two lands*
> *And all that you created.*

You may be distant, but your rays are here on earth.

When the sun had risen, we wandered blissfully in the garden. "There is no joy so pure as the joy of worship." His face glowed. But even then, Akhenaten's life was not free of pain. His failure in military training embittered him. "My father will not forgo his desire to make me a warrior, Meri-Ra," he complained. Then he looked in the gold-framed mirror and said, "Alas! Neither beauty nor strength."

The death of his older brother Tuthmosis left him with a scar in his soul. Only a deeper wound, the death of his beloved daughter Meketaten, made the pain of his childhood loss bearable. How he cried for his brother. Death became a mystery, a terrible question that confronted him mercilessly.

"What is death, Meri-Ra?" he asked. I remained quiet, avoiding the conventional answers he detested. "Even Ay does not know," he continued. "Only the sun rises again after it has gone. Tuthmosis will never return."

Thus was the eternal war he waged on weakness and grief. He set himself on a path, like the rays of the sun, promising a bright day every morning. Then one beautiful morning I met him in his place of retreat. He was rather pale, but there was something about the fixed gaze of his eyes that made him look fearless.

"The sun is nothing, Meri-Ra," he said without returning my greeting. I did not understand what he meant. He pulled me down beside him on the straw mat and continued, "Heed my words, Meri-Ra, for I speak the truth. Last night I was intoxicated with ecstasy. The darkness of the night was my companion, so intimate, like a lovely bride. I was entranced with longing for the Creator. And there, across a thousand visions, the truth revealed itself to me, more apparent than anything seen with the eye. I heard a voice sweeter than the scent of flowers: 'Fill thy soul with my breath,' it said. 'Renounce what I have not granted thee. I am the Creator, I am the stream from which life flows. I am love, peace, and joy. Fill thy heart with my love, quench the thirst of all the tortured souls on earth.'"

He was radiant with excitement, dazzling.

"Do not fear the truth, Meri-Ra," he continued, "for in the truth you will find happiness."

"What splendid light," I murmured breathlessly.

"Come, live with me in the truth," he urged me.

I sat upright. "I am with you, my Prince, until the very end."

Akhenaten became the first priest of the One and Only God. He became my teacher and spiritual guide, eager to answer my questions even before I asked. One day I said, "I believe in your God."

"Rejoice!" he cried. "You shall be the first priest in his temple."

Akhenaten declared his new faith to a few of his close companions. When he married Nefertiti—and he delighted in marriage—he was most pleased that she, too, believed in the One and Only. He did not begin the denunciation of other deities until later. During his father's rule, Akhenaten did not have the power to do what he liked. Later, when he became king, his attacks came progressively. At first he renounced all the deities. Then he abolished their worship, confiscated the temples, and allotted their patrimonies to the poor. In Akhetaten I became the high priest of the One God. When my king decided to close the temples, I warned him, "You are challenging a power that has prevailed through the ages and across the land, from Nubia to the sea."

"The priests are swindlers," he said confidently. "They live off propagating superstition in order to exploit the poor and extort their daily bread. Their temples are brothels, and there is nothing they hold sacred but their carnal desires."

I discovered then that within his feeble body Akhenaten possessed a power that no one had guessed at. His courage exceeded that of Haremhab and Mae, who had reputations for bravery. To everyone else he was an enigma, but to me he was as clear as the sun. He exhausted himself in the love of his God and devoted his life to the service of the One and Only, regardless of the consequences. I did not find his performance during the memorable tour of the empire surprising at all. Nor was I surprised that he kept to his message of love and peace even in the most extreme circumstances. He dwelled in the expanse of God's empire and lived by his command. For Akhenaten, the shrewdness of politicians and the power of military men was of no significance. It was only the truth that concerned him. They accused him of living an illusion, and of madness.

The truth, however, was that they were the ones who

dwelled on the illusions of a corrupt world; they were a raving mob. Indeed the throne was the least of his concerns. I remember how he became morose when he was summoned from his tour to claim the throne after his father died. "I wonder if the duties of the throne will keep me away from my God?" he asked sullenly.

"But my King," I replied eagerly, "it is but a divine purpose to put the power of the throne in the service of God, as your forefathers have done for their false deities."

"You speak the truth, Meri-Ra." He appeared relieved. "They sacrificed the lives of poor peasants to their gods. I shall slay evil and offer it to my God. Thus I shall be God's instrument to break the shackles of those who have no power."

He ascended the throne to fight the most fierce of wars. He fought for the happiness of people, as his God commanded him. During that war he proved that he was stronger and more enduring than Tuthmosis III.

He proclaimed his religion in the provinces. People were exhilarated. They received him with flowers and love.

He was determined to renew every day the faith of his own men, those who were closest to him. They would stand before the throne, and when they had finished discussing the affairs of the nation with Nefertiti, Akhenaten would talk with them about religion, so that he was certain that they were deserving of God's bounty.

Meri-Ra was silent for a while. He heaved a loud sigh then continued.

Then clouds of grief came, one after the other, driven by winds of spite, within the country and from outside. Each man faced up to them according to the strength of his faith, and although some of them faltered, my King was not distraught. "God will not let me down," he said. One day in the temple he asked derisively, "My men advise me to be moderate, and my God commands me to uphold the faith. Whom should I follow, Meri-Ra?" The question required no answer.

Haremhab came to meet me in the temple when matters were at their worst. "You are the high priest of the One God, Meri-Ra, the closest of all men to the king," he said.

"It is but a gift from God, bestowed upon his servant," I replied, anticipating what he was about to request.

"The situation demands a change in policy," he started.

I replied firmly, "Heed only the voice of God."

He frowned. "I hoped we might have a reasonable discussion."

"Only true believers are capable of a reasonable discussion," I replied.

When I learned about the men's decision to abandon the king under the pretense of protecting his life, I said to Ay, "I cannot accept a return to heathen ways."

My King refused to compromise. It is not that he did not care about the welfare of the country, for he, too, had his plan to avoid civil war. He had intended to confront his people and the rebels alone. He was confident that he had the ability to guide them afresh to the faith. But by then, the men were convinced that he was going to be killed, and that if they did not leave they would soon pay the price with their own lives. Everyone deserted him. Armed soldiers came to take me. The guards who were left with Akhenaten were ordered to stop him if he attempted to venture out of his palace. Thus they prevented him from confronting people. He became a prisoner in his palace. Even Nefertiti left him. I cannot imagine that she left him willingly; she, too, I should think, was carried away by force. He was filled with grief for the faith that he had spent his life trying to plant in people's hearts. Then we received news that he was ill, and shortly after, he died. Actually, I doubt that his death was caused by illness. I believe that the foul hands of the priests of Amun had finally found their way into his pure, precious soul. He died without knowing that I never wanted to leave his side.

———

Once more Meri-Ra was silent. He gazed at me for a long time, then he said, "Akhenaten did not and will not die. For he has found the eternal truth. The day will come when he will be victorious. He heard the voice of God promise that He would never forsake him."

Meri-Ra reached over to open a drawer beside him. He produced a scroll of papyrus and handed it to me. "This is a record of all his religious teachings and his songs," he said. "Study it, young man. Perhaps your truth-loving heart will find some solace in his words. You did not start this journey for no reason."

M a e

————

I went to meet Mae in Rano Kolboura on the border where he lived in a tent among his Border Army soldiers. During Akhenaten's time he had been commander of the armed forces, and had deservedly maintained his position in the new era. He was an older man, of giant stature and solemn features. He struck me as rather vain. He read my father's letter and appeared keen to talk. I suppose I had provided him with a chance to vent his feelings, isolated as he was in this remote place.

————

The heretic! A vile, low-born man who humbled the strongest of men by his perversity. The drums of war were silenced, the flags of glory lowered; the sound of music ascended from the throne of the pharaohs. I, commander of armed forces, was forced to remain idle as the empire was torn to pieces and gradually fell into the hands of the enemies and the rebels. When our faithful friends and allies cried for help, I could not aid them and their cries vanished into thin air. Because of Akhenaten we lost our military honor. We became an object of derision, and an easy prey for bandits.

Fortunately, I was never one of his close friends. But duty required that I go to Akhetaten occasionally. On every visit I wondered how such a distorted creature was able to deceive men like Ay, Haremhab, and Nakht. I have always been loyal to the gods and traditions of my country, and was extremely angry the day I heard about his alleged new god. When Akhenaten ordered the closing of the temples I was certain that a terrible curse would befall us all. During a visit to Thebes the high priest came to see me in my palace one night.

"I hope that I am not embarrassing you with this visit," he said.

"It is an honor and my palace is at your command." He seemed astonished at my openness.

He thanked me then said, "You are redeemed, Mae. People have lost their solace. They used to take refuge in their gods, made them offerings and received their blessings. In times of trouble they hurried to the priests for guidance in life and the hereafter. Poor souls, look at them now, lost like stray sheep."

"What good is complaining?" I asked irritably. "Is it not our duty to rid the country of his madness?"

"If we do as you advise, we shall face a crushing war," he replied after a moment's thought.

"Is there no solution then?"

"To convince the men closest to him."

"A far-fetched hope."

"We must not resort to the desperate measures you propose before we exhaust all other options."

"I can promise you the support of the armed forces when you need it," I said.

Winning over the men in Akhenaten's chamber, however, would have required more time than we had. Civil war had already begun to threaten the country. Nothing could be done but to salvage what remained beneath the ruins.

People asked themselves why the sweet dream had turned into a nightmare. I believe that a tragedy was bound to happen, and that its secret lay in the weakness of the heretic, his weakness of mind and body. His mother spoiled him and sheltered him from the reality of his sickness. Consequently he was excruciatingly jealous when he compared himself with his more distinguished peers, like Haremhab, Nakht, and Bek. The contrast was demeaning. He concealed his shame behind a curtain of feminine meekness and sweetness, and secretly nurtured a desire to destroy every single strong figure, be it god or priest, so that he could be the sole power. Some of the men recognized his weakness of spirit, and found in it a stepping stone to their ambitions. They were quick to join his religion, not out of fear of his power or faith in his religion, not out of fear of his power or faith in his god, but out of greed. His weakness was an invitation to the greedy and the ill-willed. They sang with him in the temple, then turned around and stripped the poor of what little they had. When the people began to rebel, he sent them messages of love instead of the army. At last, when death threatened them, they abandoned him and joined forces with his enemies, loaded with loot. That is why when the high priest of Amun wanted to negotiate, I protested.

"You must not warn them," I said. "Do not go to Akhetaten. Let me and my forces take them by surprise and destroy them, so that justice will be done."

Toto supported me enthusiastically, but the high priest opted for peaceful negotiations and ruled against any bloodshed. "Our losses are already insurmountable," he said. "We do not want other complications."

I understood the priest's misgivings. He feared that if he gave me permission to attack and I was triumphant, I would hoard the merit of saving the country, and thus have a strong claim to the throne. The high priest would then be faced with a powerful king, and would be unable to act outside the boundaries I set for him. Because of this, he decided to entrust the throne to the young Tutankhamun. Now they all circle like vultures around the throne—the high priest, Ay, and Haremhab. Nevertheless, Egypt is far better off today than it was during the heretic's reign. Akhenaten was left to die, bitter and alone. As for Nefertiti, she awaits her final day among the ruins of the heathen city.

———

Mae's silence announced that he had finished. "What about Nefertiti, Chief Commander? I should like to learn more about her," I asked.

He answered dismissively, "A beautiful woman created to be a whore. Her course was charted so that she could practice her sport of seducing men, from the throne. Do not believe what you hear about her competence as queen. If any of it were true, the country would not have fallen during her reign into that pit of corruption and destruction. She too abandoned him at the last minute, when he had lost what little power he ever had. But she failed to climb onto the other ship in time."

Maho

────────

I visited Maho in his village in south Thebes. He was chief of police in Akhetaten during the time of Akhenaten. Now he subsisted on farming. Maho was forty years old when I met him, well built, with coarse features and mournful eyes. When he finished reading my father's letter he put his hands behind his head and remained in that position a while, collecting his memories. "The spring of joy dried up when Akhenaten left our world," he started. "O Egypt, may the gods forgive you."

────────

I was merely a guard in the palace the first time Akhenaten addressed me. For someone of my status, to speak directly to the prince was like a dream. I often saw him from a distance in the garden. One morning he approached my post curiously, as though he had discovered for the first time that I existed. I felt myself turn to stone before him. He stared at me until I felt his gaze running with my blood and recurring with my breath.

"What is your name?" he asked.

"Maho."

"Where do you come from?"

"The village of Fina."

"And your family's work?"

"Farming."

"Why did Haremhab appoint you to the guards?"

"I do not know."

"He selects his men on the basis of courage." My heart jumped with happiness but I said nothing. "You are an honest young man, Maho." I could hardly contain my joy. "Will you accept my friendship?" he asked.

"It is an honor I do not deserve," I stammered, trying to overcome my daze.

"We shall meet often, my friend."

Unbelievable as it may sound, that was precisely what happened between me and the crown prince the first time he acknowledged me. That was how Akhenaten selected his men. Indeed he spoke to me briefly whenever he saw me in the palace garden. I followed his life from afar. First I heard about his worship of Aten, then about the One and Only God. I often heard him singing beautiful hymns to his God. My heart was entirely open to him. It was as though his love was a spell that bound me to him eternally. I admit that I understood only a little of what he said. For a long time I was rather confused by this mysterious, invisible god of his, who loves people and does not punish them. I did not stop believing in

Amun, but I believed in the other god, too, because of my love for Akhenaten. He was the most compassionate of people. He harmed neither man nor beast, never stained his hands with blood, and never judged anyone, regardless of what harm they did. When he ascended the throne after his father's death, he summoned me, and said, "I shall not force you to do anything you do not wish to, Maho. You will earn a living, whatever happens. Do you want to declare your faith in the One and Only God?"

"I do, my King, and I declare my readiness to die in his cause," I replied without hesitation.

"You will be chief of police," he said calmly, "and no one will ask you to lay down your life."

I was prepared to fight the priests, even though I had been taught to love and respect them since I was a young boy. Yet for all the time I worked in Akhenaten's forces, I never struck at anyone—except once, and then I acted without his permission.

"From now on," he said to me the day of my appointment, "let your weapon be like an ornament. Discipline people with love, the way I taught you. Remember, what love cannot cure, fear will not correct."

Whenever we captured a thief we simply retrieved what he had stolen. Then, we sent him to work on the plantations and taught him the words of love and peace. When we caught someone who had killed, we sent him to work in the mines. There, too, they learned about the new religion, when they were not working. Many times we were betrayed in return for our generosity, but

Akhenaten never lost heart. "Soon you will see the tree of love heavy with fruit," he insisted.

Akhenaten spent his day praying in solitude, and singing his hymns at the temple. Then he spoke to the people from the terrace of his palace. He and Nefertiti rode through Akhetaten in their royal carriage. They were never accompanied by guards. Sometimes they got down from the carriage to greet the masses of people that gathered around them. The old traditions that had separated the common people from the pharaohs were no longer exercised. Wherever they went, they called for the love and worship of the One and Only God.

One morning a young man in my force reported, "I heard troublesome whispers among the elite."

It was the beginning of the end. Corruption spread among the civil servants, the peasants suffered, and rebellion swept the empire. Deception and malice flowed with the water of the Nile. I feared how grief might affect the king, but in fact the turbulence made his enthusiasm and determination grow. He was confident of victory. He never doubted that love would prevail, as though the darkness had descended only to usher in a greater light. In those dismal days, the priests sent a criminal to take the life of the king. He lurked in the darkness of Akhenaten's retreat, and would have succeeded had I not stopped him with an arrow in his chest. My King then realized the extent of the danger. He became increasingly sullen, staring into the face of the criminal as he gasped his last breath. "You did your duty, Maho," the king said reluctantly.

"I will sacrifice my life to save my King," I said.

"Couldn't you have captured him alive?" he asked in the same tone.

"No, my King," I replied honestly.

He said sadly, "The priests conspired to commit a wicked crime; they failed, and we have fallen into evil."

"Some evil can be fought only with the sword," I replied.

"This is what they have always said, since before Menes united the two kingdoms. But did they overcome evil?" Then he cried, as though suddenly inspired, "Await the time when East and West shall be seen in one outpouring of light."

But the light did not come. Things continued to deteriorate. Men revealed themselves to be hollow ghosts. They fell away like dried leaves yielding to the autumn winds. They had neither faith nor loyalty. They distorted the truth and held fast to falsehood until the last minute. They abandoned him under the pretense of protecting his life.

Haremhab ordered me to leave Akhenaten with my men. I was unable to dissuade him. I was not permitted to see Akhenaten once before I left, not even to say good-bye.

I returned to Thebes with a heartache that has never left me to this very day. I was relieved of my duties, as were many of his loyal men, and returned to my village to mourn him. I received news that the king was a prisoner in his palace, then that he had fallen ill and died. I was certain that they killed him.

How could such a beautiful dream end so quickly? Why did God forsake him? What meaning is there to life now that he has left us?

———

Maho gave in to his grief and remained silent. I, too, sat silently, respectful of his sentiments. When a moment had passed, I asked him, "How would you describe Akhenaten in a few words?" He seemed startled by my question. "He was the pure essence of sweetness and benevolence. But I cannot say more about him than the facts I have told you."

"And Nefertiti?"

"She was beauty and brilliance combined."

I prompted him after a moment's hesitation. "So much has been said about her."

"I can tell you, as chief of police, that I did not have a single incident recorded against her. I did, however, notice the lustful looks that Haremhab, Nakht, and Mae gave her. But I can assure you that she didn't encourage anyone to overstep their boundaries."

"Why do you suppose she left him?"

He seemed bewildered. "It is a mystery I have failed to understand."

"It seems to me that you have stopped believing in your king's god."

"I no longer believe in any god."

Nakht

———

Nakht was from an old, noble family. He was in his forties, a man of average height and a fair complexion
flushed with a tint of rose. He was strikingly composed,
more so than any other person I have met. He was the
minister of Akhenaten's chamber. He did not occupy a
position in the new era, but he was summoned occasionally for his expertise. I met him in his home province,
Dekma, in the middle Delta. He welcomed me, alluding
to the old affiliation between our families. Then he told
me the story, leaving out some of the things I already
knew.

———

I confess that I am not a happy man. I failed to assume
the responsibilities of my position. Thus I not only for-
feited any chance of ascending the throne, but I also saw
the empire collapse before my very eyes. I retired from

political and public life, but I shall always have regrets. I often ask myself, "What kind of being was my king, Akhenaten?" Or should I say "the heretic" now?

I was one of his friends from boyhood, like Haremhab and Bek. I could speak at great length about his unusually feminine features, his feeble body, and his generally strange appearance. But despite all that, he was able to make us love him and admire his intelligence and precocious maturity.

Certainly Akhenaten had his flaws. I was the first to discover a grave defect in his character—he was not in the least concerned with the operative matters of government. Indeed they bored him greatly. He looked on ironically as his father went about the daily routine on which the traditions of the throne were based—waking up at the same hour, bathing, eating, praying, conferring with the men of his cabinet, then visiting the temple. "What enslavement," Akhenaten said. He trifled with tradition like a spoilt child amusing himself by breaking expensive items. But when it came to mystical questions of life and death and the mysterious powers of the universe, he was very ambitious. He became more determined in pursuing these ambitions after his brother Tuthmosis died. He suffered the loss of his companion, and decided to strike mercilessly against any suffering. His exuberant imagination paved the way for him, but ultimately led him to disaster. Perhaps we all had our fanciful visions, but we knew that it was merely imagination. Akhenaten, however, wanted to make his fantasies a reality. As a result, he was accused of madness and idiocy. No. He was not mad and he was not a fool—though he was not normal either.

At a very young age he became a burden to his father and the priests of Amun. For us he was an enigma. To question the precedence of Amun, worship Aten, then invent a god that was the sole source of creation in the universe, was beyond what we could fathom. I did not doubt his sincerity, but I was also certain that he was mistaken. He never lied, but he did not hear the voice of a god. It was his own heart that spoke. It might have been more acceptable if the one who claimed the prophecy had been a priest, but to be the crown prince of the throne of Egypt is a different matter. He began to tell people about his prophecy, about the god of love, peace, and joy. During his father's reign, Akhenaten was powerless, but he was determined to do away with all the traditional gods and their temples as soon as he was able. When he became king, the dream was superimposed on reality. The balance of life was disrupted and tragedy threatened. When he ascended the throne, he invited us to join his new religion. I was of the opinion we should decline.

"Perhaps if he found himself alone he would renounce his cause," I said to Haremhab.

"I am afraid he would find other people, with neither morals nor experience, and they would haul the country to its destruction."

"But couldn't the same thing happen at our hands?"

Haremhab smiled sarcastically. "He is far too weak to disregard our opinion." Then he shrugged his shoulders and muttered, "He has nothing but words; we have power."

And so I declared my faith in his religion. He appointed me minister of chamber and my fears subsided. I met him every day in Thebes or in Akhetaten to deliberate matters of government, finance, security, and water resources. He would remain silent while the queen and I conferred. Nefertiti's aptitude for politics was beyond imagination; she was a powerful presence on the throne of Egypt. As for the king, he spoke only of his god and his message and gave instructions that served his religion. When Akhenaten decided to abolish the traditional religions, I warned him of the consequences.

"Your faith is still weak, Nakht," he said reproachfully.

We walked together to the terrace and stood before the crowd that had gathered in the concourse. He had the power of magic in the souls of his people. He announced his decision with a frightening determination. Cries of adulation filled the air. I felt as though I was nonexistent and that the feeble creature beside me possessed a mysterious power never encountered before. Despite Nefertiti's shrewdness, she submitted herself to her husband and enthused about his message as if it was her own. I was rather surprised by her position. This woman is either his spiritual partner, I thought, or the most insidious being humanity has ever known. I believe that what had secured such success for him from the beginning was that no one dared to contradict him but me. Haremhab did not utter a word in opposition until the crisis was at its height. As for Ay, he feigned devoutness and dedication to the new god. If I blame anyone, I would accuse Ay of deception and ill-intent. He contrived a scheme to take the throne of Egypt. As the appointed teacher of the crown prince, Ay knew Akhenaten's weaknesses. He was the one who converted him to Aten and imbued him with the idea of the One God. Akhenaten's marriage to Nefertiti was devised by Ay as a part of his scheme, despite his awareness that the prince was an impotent man. Thus he became the king's father-in-law and his counselor, known in Egypt as the Sage. He induced him to abolish the traditional gods and to appropriate their temples, in order to sow the seeds of dissension between him and the priests. He hoped that the strife would either force Akhenaten to abdicate the throne or culminate in his assassination. Ay was well aware of the considerations that made him a candidate for the throne. He was father-in-law of the king and sage of Egypt. Because of his old age, his reign would be short-lived. He therefore posed no significant threat to those who coveted the throne for themselves. Perhaps he even planned to marry his own daughter to substantiate the succession, and so that she could continue as queen of Egypt. You must understand that my opinion is not based on my personal impressions alone. I had private and reliable sources that provided me with indisputable evidence. Yet his scheme failed. There were two factors that stopped him from succeeding. First there was the people's loyalty to the pharaoh. And then, at the critical moment, the priests appointed Tutankhamun king. But I believe Ay still ruminates on his old dream.

I could not tell anyone what I thought, but I continued to offer my advice to the king.

"My King," I said, "your God is undoubtedly the only true God. But you must permit the people to worship their own gods. Build a temple for the Only Creator in every province and he will have the last victory. Spare the country all this needless turmoil."

But it would have been easier to move a pyramid than to move Akhenaten from his position.

"Your faith is still weak, Nakht," was all he said.

"To defend one's faith is a right that does not counter love and peace," I insisted.

"Even the most wicked people will yield to the power of love, for love is stronger than the sword."

When the storm clouds gathered, I called a closed meeting with the high priest of Amun and Commander Mae.

"We must act now before we lose what is left of our honor." They eyed me with curiosity and I continued, "Let the priests stop stirring up trouble. Then Mae will lead his forces to save the empire."

"Move without orders from the pharaoh?" Mae asked.

"Yes," I replied calmly.

Of the three of us, the priest was the strongest. He asked, "And then what?"

"When Mae is victorious, the king will be forced to declare freedom of worship."

"I must disagree," the high priest said. "That's not a good plan. The leaders of the troops might rebel against Mae if he ordered them to move without a royal decree." Then he frowned and his face reddened. "Your loyalty is to your king, Nakht, not us. You must have learned about our success in the provinces and decided to hinder our progress with your inane proposition."

Angered by the priest's stab, I left them. I was certain now that everyone merely wanted to serve their own purposes. Egypt was in the hands of villains. They were all responsible for the destruction of the country, whether they were with the king or against him. Perhaps Akhenaten was the least to blame. They used him for their benefit. When he was no longer of any use, they wanted to depose him and claim the throne. Because of his trusting nature he believed their lies. Then a power that no one anticipated rose up from within him and swept them swiftly along for a time, until it crashed against the hard rock of reality. Then each one headed for the life raft, leaving their visionary victim to sink alone, wondering why his God had forsaken him. They tore the masks off their faces, most of all Nefertiti and her father Ay. Each of them took a different path, but none was dealt their retribution. Except the poor heretic, and to some extent Nefertiti, when the priests did not accept her false penitence. As for Egypt, it lay sore with wounds, bleeding under the weight of our blunders.

————

The minister was silent for a long time. Then he mumbled in deep sadness, "This is a story of innocence, of deception, and infinite grief."

Bento

Bento was Akhenaten's personal physician. Indeed, when I met him, he still occupied the position of personal physician of the pharaoh in Tutankhamun's palace. Bento was sixty years old, with a noble bearing and marks of Nubian descent. When I visited him in his beautiful palace at the center of Thebes, I found him to be a man of serene nature and soft voice, yet extremely energetic. His clothes were exquisitely tasteful. Gathering his memories, Bento began.

Today, Akhenaten is known only as "the heretic." But despite all that was said about him, my heart still fills with love at the mention of his name. What a life he created for himself! Did Akhenaten really live among us? Did he really devote his life to love? Why, then, all the malice and hatred that was left behind? Whenever I think of him I remember how, when he was a young boy, he aroused the concern of all those who knew him. The Great Queen Tiye would often ask me, "Why is Akhenaten so frail, Bento?"

I remember my confusion in trying to answer. Akhenaten had no particular ailment. But he was thin and feeble, and, unlike his brother Tuthmosis, he was prey to every malady that came his way. He did not like sport, nor was he keen on maintaining a good diet. I often prayed to Thoth, the god of science, asking him to advise me on Akhenaten. Yet all my attempts were to no avail. Thoth's amulets had no effect on him, and herbs blessed by Isis did nothing to help his sickly body. I became extremely worried when, during the khamsin winds, he fell ill and his brother soon contracted the same disease. They were both confined to one room when the queen said to me, "Look, Bento, their faces are so yellow, and their stomachs feel like stone. Neither of them has relieved himself in days."

I examined them carefully. "They have a temperature and their stomachs are bloated. Give them a drink that will ease their bowels. Then mix some sweet, fermented malt water with flour and leave it to infuse overnight. Let that be their only food for four days."

Before four days had passed the strong Tuthmosis died and the feeble brother was spared. Akhenaten wandered about the palace, grieving, looking for his brother.

"You left my brother to die," he protested when he saw me. Then he looked at his father and continued, "When I become pharaoh, I will kill death."

"Could Tuthmosis come back for just one day?" he asked me once.

"Pray to the gods who spared your soul, Akhenaten, for there is no return from death, and we shall all die in time," I replied.

"Why?" he insisted.

"Akhenaten," I said softly, "let us hear that song you sang with your brother."

Our loved ones left us
Only words to remember.
O saddened hearts,
Live not in grief,
For Osiris shall hear no pleas,
Nor will wailing
Bring back the dead.

For a long time sadness was his only companion, so much so that I thought he outdid even his mother in mourning his brother. As I was treating him once, he asked, "Why all this effort if we are going to die anyhow?" I smiled and continued my work. He said, "You smile as though you were immortal."

I replied, to avoid his pestering, "Ask your tutor Ay."

"Ay doesn't know any more than you," he said scornfully.

The maturity of his mind, in one so young and delicate, made a deep impression on me. I followed his spiritual adventures keenly, and was filled with admiration. He had astounding qualities that one could not fathom;

he had the power to defy any force that challenged him. Despite his physical weakness, he had exceptional perseverance. He barely slept. Instead, he prayed constantly like a priest, and read like a sage. He never wearied of asking questions or debating. What, I wondered, would destiny hold in store for him if one day he sat on the throne of his forefathers? His father, King Amenhotep III, was so concerned that he once said, "The boy is worthy of anything but the throne."

One day I noticed him glaring angrily at his father. "You understand matters beyond your age," I said, "but you still do not realize your father's greatness."

He replied irritably, "I cannot bear the way he gobbles his food."

He was repulsed by those who were driven by carnal desires. I used to believe a healthy body was essential for a healthy soul, but he proved that the opposite was also true. I learned from him that the soul may lend a weak body power beyond its physical capabilities.

"You pay so much attention to the body, as if it were everything, when in fact the real strength lies in the soul," he said. "The body is a poor frame, sordid and amoral. It can fail and collapse with only an insect's sting. But the soul is immortal." Then he cried out, as if he had completely forgotten my existence, "I do not know what I want, but I know that I am full of desire. Oh how dreary is the long night!"

He would sit silently in the darkness awaiting the sunrise, and when the light came he would be glowing with happiness. Until one day he heard the voice of the One God with the first rays of sunlight. I realized then that

Akhenaten was no gentle spring breeze, but a winter storm. Thebes knew no peace thereafter.

The king and queen summoned me. "What is the meaning of that voice he heard, Bento?" Tiye asked.

I was bewildered. "Perhaps the sage Ay is more suited to answer your question, my Queen."

"The queen asked you in your capacity as a doctor," the king said severely.

"I know no mind as sound as his, Your Majesty," I replied sincerely.

"Is he mocking us then?"

"He is the most earnest man I know."

"So you have no explanation for it."

"That is the truth, Your Majesty."

"Do you think his mind is sound?" he asked with a scowl.

"Yes, Your Majesty."

"Could it be the voice of some evil force?"

"Decipher his words, for only they bear the answer to your question."

He cried angrily, "The answer is in the storms that will hit us when the priests learn of his absurdity."

When Akhenaten married Nefertiti, everyone hoped that in marriage his religious ardor would be restrained, and that he would begin to have a more realistic vision. But the wife, too, became a priestess. Together, they walked the path of the One and Only. No power on earth could stop them. Amenhotep III died and Akhenaten, bearing the message of the One Creator, succeeded him. We knew that in his reign something of grave significance was bound to happen; we were frightened to predict what it might be. Like the others, I was given the choice of either adopting his faith or living my life however I wished away from his palace. I did not hesitate and declared my faith in his God. The thought of being away from him was unbearable. Besides, I did love his God and secretly considered him the master of all gods. But I also kept my old faith in the other deities, especially Thoth, the god of science, whose talismans I used to treat people's maladies. Then there was the new city, Akhetaten, the marvelous city of the One God. We moved to it all together, an assembly of joyful people singing blissfully. The king was entranced, his face beaming with ecstasy.

"Here we are, O Mighty God, humble and transient in your pure city. O Great One, we enter your home, which has never known any god but you."

At first we were so happy that we wished we were created immortal to live forever in that paradise. Every morning I compared what I heard in the temple of the One God to the liturgy of the old gods and the rituals of the Book of the Dead. I became certain beyond doubt that a stream of divine light was filling us with pure happiness. The first winds of trouble came with the death of the beloved princess Meketaten.

"Bento, save her. She is the love of my life," Akhenaten pleaded.

When the beautiful princess passed away, the king and queen wept a flood of tears. He blamed his God until Meri-Ra said, "Do not anger God with your tears."

Upon hearing the high priest, Akhenaten's wailing grew louder. No one knew if it was out of grief or guilt. Perhaps both.

"It is the sorcery of the priests of Amun," Nefertiti cried. She repeated the same words every time she bore a daughter and the chance of a male heir was lost once more. Akhenaten shared her pain.

"Bento," he asked, "can you help us bear a son?"

"I try my best, Your Majesty."

"Do you believe in the sorcery of the priests?"

"We certainly should not underestimate it," I replied reluctantly.

He meditated for a moment. "God will persevere, and his joy will fill the universe. But we, his humble creation, shall never be rid of our little sorrows," he said mournfully. Because of his faith he was always able to elevate himself from grief to the summit of the holy truth where the brilliant light of God inundated his soul.

When the tension grew inside Egypt and on its borders, the high priest of Amun sent me a secret messenger.

"Can I trust you with saving the country from the dreadful fate that looms over it?" he asked, after reminding me of my vow in the temple of Amun.

I realized instantly that the high priest wanted me to use my role as the king's physician to kill him. I replied, "My profession does not condone treachery."

I met with Maho, the chief of police, and asked him to step up security, particularly among the cooks in the palace.

––––––––

Bento was silent for a while, seeking some rest from these wearisome memories. I remembered some of the conflicting reports I had heard about Akhenaten's sexuality, but doubted that Bento would allude to it. Since I was very curious, I had to ask. "Akhenaten's body and features had the attributes of both male and female," he said. "But, as a man, he was capable of loving and pro-creating." Then my lips trembled with a pressing ques-tion. After a moment of hesitation I mustered up all my courage and asked, "Have you heard what they say about his relationship with his mother?" Bento scowled and said, "Of course I have, just like you. But I always dismissed it as malicious fabrication." He stopped for a moment, looking increasingly troubled, then continued, "The fact is that Akhenaten was a very special being, far too good for any of us to understand. He was a vision-ary, promising a paradise irreconcilable with human nature. He confronted people with their mediocrity and provoked their deepest fears. So they pounced on him with animal anger and desperation."

Encouraged by his openness, I continued, "What do you think of Nefertiti?"

"A great queen who has earned her greatness."

"And how do you explain her desertion of Akhen-aten?"

"I have only one explanation. She could not endure the blows that poured down on them; she felt helpless and took flight." Then he continued.

———

The tragedy came to a terrible end when Akhenaten's men decided to abandon him. I asked Haremhab to let me stay with him as his physician. He told me that the priests would send their own physician to tend him. But he allowed me to examine him for the last time before I left. I went to the palace at once. It was empty apart from him and a few slaves and guards that the priests had appointed.

I found him in his usual solitude, praying, singing gently:

Lord of the beautiful, O Beautiful One,
With your love hearts beat
And birds trill.
You dwell within me, O Lord.
No other has known you
But your son,
Akhenaten.

When he finished his prayer, he looked at me and smiled. I looked away to hide the tears in my eyes.

"How were you able to come, Bento?" he asked.

"Haremhab gave me permission to examine you before I left."

"I am in excellent health," he said calmly.

"All the loyal ones were forced to leave," I said, my voice tremulous with feeling.

"I know who was forced and who chose to leave." The smile never left his face.

I bowed down and kissed his hand. "It pains me that you must remain alone."

"I am not alone. Have faith, Bento," he said calmly. Then he continued with an invigorating determination,

"They think that my God and I are defeated. But he never betrays nor does he accept defeat."

I cried so much that when I left the palace my eyes were like firebrands. I was certain that the physician they sent him would kill the most noble soul that has ever inhabited a human body. Since the time I left Akhetaten, I have been immersed in inescapable loneliness.

Nefertiti

I was allowed to enter Akhetaten only with special permission from General Haremhab. There were security checks at short intervals all along the bank of the Nile. A soldier escorted me across the northern quarter of the city from the harbor to the palace of the imprisoned queen. I was barraged by a host of emotions that left me stranded between sadness and wonder. The once glorious streets of Akhetaten had disappeared beneath heaps of dust and the dried leaves of withered trees. The grand doors of the palaces were closed like eyelids on tearful eyes. The palaces were collapsed, the fences fallen. The gardens had lost their colors and were left with the remains of trees shriveled like mummies. A heavy silence covered the city. In the center were the ruins of the temple of the One and Only God, where once the sweetest and holiest hymns were sung.

It was early afternoon when I reached the far end of

the northern quarter. The queen's palace towered in the distance, set in a lush and colorful garden. My heart pounded when I glimpsed the only open window in the palace. It was the middle of autumn and the Nile was still in flood. Its mud-red water had filled the palace lake. My heart beat faster as I approached the end of my journey, as though the entire purpose of my quest was to meet this woman in her solitude.

I was ushered into a small, elegant room. The walls were inscribed with holy texts. In the center of the room there was an ebony chair with golden arms and legs, each sculpted in the form of a lion.

Finally I saw her, a vision, coming toward me gracefully in a white, flowing dress. She was elegant and beautiful. Her back was unbowed by forty years of grief and misfortune. I waited until she was settled in her chair, then she gestured to me and I sat before her. The beauty of her serene eyes was overcast by a shadow of weariness. She praised my father, then asked me bitterly, "And how do you find the city of light?"

I realized that I had been staring at her, captivated by her beauty. Abashed, I lowered my gaze, and remained silent.

"You must have heard a lot of tales about Akhenaten and me," she said. "Now you can hear the whole truth."

———

I grew up with a passion for true knowledge that was nurtured by the learnedness of my father, Ay. I lost my real mother when I was only one year old. But I did not feel that loss, for in Tey I found a compassionate, loving mother, and not merely a stepmother. She gave me a splendid, happy childhood. Even after she had my sister Mutnedjmet, her feelings toward me did not change. She was a wise woman. At first, Mutnedjmet and I were loving sisters. Because I was better at most things than Mutnedjmet, she became jealous and built up a fair share of resentment. But that only became evident much later. Tey, however, remained impartial, at least on the surface. I was quite grateful, and when the time came for me to reward her I appointed her the queen's matron and gave her the status of princess. One day, my father returned home with a holy man, one of those who are endowed with the gift of foretelling the future. He read both our fortunes, my sister's and mine.

"These girls shall sit on the throne of Egypt," he said.

"Both of them?" said my father, astounded.

"The two of them," the man assured him.

For some time we faltered between our faith in the holy man and the peculiarity of his prophecy.

"Perhaps one of us will be first and the other will be her successor," I laughed.

For some mysterious reason Tey was not pleased with what I said. "Shall we forget about this prophecy and leave the future to the gods?" she said sharply.

We tried to forget. But every so often the prophecy seemed to cast its shadow upon us, until things began to take an unexpected course and it was fulfilled before our very eyes. The first time I heard of Akhenaten was through my father, when he was appointed tutor to the crown prince. Father used to speak of Akhenaten's wisdom and maturity during our family gatherings.

"Akhenaten is an unusual person," he once said. "He

criticizes the priests and the deities and no longer believes in any god but Aten."

Unlike my mother and sister, I was rather intrigued and drawn to what I heard. For I, too, loved Aten and was awed by his domain that comprised both heaven and earth, while other deities abided only in the darkness of the temples.

"The prince is right, Father," I replied innocently.

My mother and sister were not pleased with my remark. Father said with a smile, "We are preparing you to be a wife, Nefertiti, not a priestess."

I cannot deny my love for motherhood and other earthly pleasures, but the truth is, I was also born to be a priestess. Eventually my father told us the news of the new god, the Sole Creator. There was an uproar and the prince was the subject of stinging talk.

"What do the king and queen think?" my mother asked.

"There is so much turmoil in the palace. I am not sure what anyone thinks or believes," my father said gloomily.

"I fear that they will blame you, as his teacher."

"He is their son. They know that he will never follow anyone, no matter how grand they are."

"He is insane," Mutnedjmet said. "He will lose his throne. Is there another heir?"

"He has only one sickly older sister."

As they talked I felt such emotion that I was afraid I would faint. To me, the crown prince represented an irresistibly attractive, fabulous story. But I did not come to any particular conviction then. One evening I overheard my father secretly reciting one of the hymns of the new god:

Lord of the beautiful, O Beautiful One,
With your love hearts beat
And birds trill.
You dwell within me, O Lord.

The words became imprinted in my heart forever, and I was elated with joy. I repeated the hymn and let its sweet nectar infuse my soul. Its words attracted me as a butterfly is drawn to light. And like the butterfly, I was burned by that light. I was filled with faith. What a beautiful and peaceful feeling it was! "My Only God," I whispered, "I believe in you eternally."

I presented myself to my father and sang the hymn.

"You were listening," he said with a frown.

I ignored his gentle reproach. "Father, what do you think of the voice he heard?"

"I do not know," he replied cautiously.

"Can he be lying?"

He thought for a moment, then said, "He never lies."

"Then it must be true."

"Perhaps what he heard was a dream," he said reluctantly.

"Father," I confessed, "I believe in the One God, the Sole Creator."

Suddenly he became pale. "Beware, Nefertiti!" he cried. "Keep your secret in your heart, until I can rid your heart of it."

Then we were invited to the palace for the Sed festival. Tey saw in it an opportunity for her daughters to meet eligible suitors. "You must be seen in the most beautiful dress," she said. But I was only anxious to see one person—he who had shown me the light of the truth. In the grand hall of the palace I met people with whom I later walked the path of life, with its sweetness and its bitterness—Haremhab, Nakht, Mae, and many others. That night, however, my heart saw no one but Akhenaten. When I first saw him, I was taken aback by his strange appearance. I had pictured him a token of perfection. Instead, he was thin and feeble. His appearance called more for pity than admiration. I admit that I was rather disappointed. But it was a momentary disappointment. I saw beyond his strange features and feeble body a spirit that was singled out by God to receive his divine love, and I secretly vowed my loyalty to this frail creature. He was seated to the right of his father, observing the dance without enthusiasm. My eyes never left him. Indeed, many people noticed that he was the focus of my attention. I shall never forget what Mutnedjmet said to me, suffering the sting of jealousy: "You have set your goal, Nefertiti. Now you will stride toward it."

I wished that he would see me. And he did. He glanced in my direction and our eyes met for the first time. He almost looked away, but his eyes moved back and he fixed his gaze upon me. I believe he was rather startled at this young woman who regarded him so intently, and with so much longing. I looked at the Great Queen Tiye and saw that she was looking at me. My heart pounded quickly, and my dreams soared in the highest sky. But I never anticipated what followed.

I returned to our palace heaving with excitement and vague desires. Mutnedjmet, however, was sullen.

"I am quite sure now," she said when we were alone

in our room. I asked her what she meant, and she continued, "He is sick and insane."

"You have only seen him from outside. You know nothing of what is in his heart."

The next day, when my father returned to the palace he told me that the Great Queen had asked to see me. His announcement shook the entire family, and we looked questioningly at each other.

"I suspect," my father continued proudly, "that the queen will appoint you one of her maids of honor."

I went to the royal palace in the company of my father. I was ushered to the queen's resting place overlooking the garden. I bowed before her until she called upon me to rise and sit on a sofa to her right.

"Your name is Nefertiti?" she said. I nodded and she continued softly, "Nefert-iti, The Beautiful One Has Come, a well-deserved name indeed." I blushed with joy. "How old are you?"

"Sixteen years, my Queen."

"You look more mature." She paused for a moment then continued, "Why do you think I summoned you?"

"A fortune beyond what I deserve."

"Well said, young woman," she smiled. "Have you acquired some education?"

"Reading, writing, poetry, history, theology, algebra, and home-making," I replied.

"What do you think of Egypt?"

"Egypt is the mother of the world, and its pharaoh the king of kings."

"Who is your most cherished deity?" she asked. I detected a keenness in her question.

"Aten, Your Majesty." I was compelled to hide the truth.

"What about Amun?"

"Amun protects the empire, but Aten circles it every day."

"One cannot control what the heart loves, but you must realize that Amun is the master of all deities."

"Indeed I do, Your Majesty."

"Tell me in all honesty," she continued, "has your heart ever known the love of a man?"

"No, Your Majesty," I replied without hesitation.

"Have you had any suitors?"

"Many asked for my hand in marriage, but my father did not consider them suitable."

She scrutinized my face for a while, then said, "You must have heard what is said about the crown prince's peculiar ideas regarding Amun and the deities. What is your honest impression?"

For the first time I was not able to reply. I remained silent until she continued in a voice laden with authority, "Speak only the truth."

"What is in the heart belongs to the heart. But the traditions established between the throne and the priests must be preserved."

"Well spoken!" she said. She appeared relieved. "Speak to me of your dream man. What is he like?"

"He has the strength of a warrior and the soul of a priest."

She laughed. "You are extremely ambitious. If you had to choose, would it be the warrior or the priest?"

"The soul is more important."

"In all honesty?"

"Yes, Your Majesty."

"You are not like other young women," she exclaimed.

"Life without faith is barren," I said.

"What is faith without life?"

"There is no faith without life, and no life without faith."

She remained silent for a while as I struggled to hide my rising excitement.

"Have you seen the crown prince?" she asked at last.

"At the Sed festival, my Queen."

"What do you think of him?"

"He has a mysterious power that distinguishes him from all other men."

"I meant, what would you think of him as a husband?"

I was silenced by the surprise. She repeated her question.

"I cannot find the words, my Queen," I replied, my voice trembling.

"Did you ever dream of being a queen?"

"My dreams have only risen as high as my humble heart."

"Doesn't the idea of the throne fascinate you?"

"It is a sky too high for my heart to fly in."

Tiye was silent for a moment. "I have chosen you as a wife for my son, the crown prince."

I closed my eyes under the intensity of my emotions. Pulling myself together again, I said, "But the prince doesn't know me, and he's not interested in me."

"But he abides by my wishes. I am his mother, and he loves me above all else," she said proudly. "It is important for me to find him a suitable wife. When I saw you I felt that you were his match. I heed my inner feelings just as much as I heed reason." I was still silenced and overwhelmed. She continued, "But you must remember that as a queen, your duties will come before all else."

"I hope to rise to your expectations, my Queen."

"Promise me your unconditional loyalty," she demanded in a penetrating voice.

"I do," I replied, unaware of the extent of my commitment.

"I am sure that you will honor your word."

I could hardly think for joy and gratitude. But the moment I bid the queen farewell and left her chamber, I felt as though my hands were bound in shackles bearing her royal signet. She was a power I could never disregard. I remembered the crown prince and knew that the greatness of his soul would not make him any more appealing as a husband. I realized that I would pay a very high price for glory.

The news was like a thunderbolt to my family. I realize, of course, that Mutnedjmet must have been very bitter, and that Tey probably shared some of that. But still it was joyful news for everyone in the family. My fortune had lifted me to the throne of Egypt, but it had also elevated them to the rank of royalty. Because of that, they showered me with kisses and good wishes. I recalled the prophecy of the old man, and shuddered as I realized that it had in part come true. I wondered if Mutnedjmet, too, would sit on the throne of Egypt. Perhaps she also remembered the prophecy and found some solace in it.

"Today, your mother will rest peacefully in her tomb," my father said when we were alone in his room.

"I hope so," I said sadly.

"You do not seem happy, my daughter," he said with a smile and a keen look.

"Reality is more frightening than imagination," I said earnestly.

"Fate could not grant you a better chance for happiness."

"Are you certain, Father, that I shall be happy?"

"The throne will bring you glory, but happiness is only in the heart."

"I believe you, Father."

"I shall pray that you will be both glorious and happy."

The marriage took place with unusual haste. The celebration held in the palace was worthy of the great king Amenhotep III and his love of worldly pleasures. Tiye took me to the golden room and sat me on the royal bed, shimmering with gold. I wore a sheer dress with my body naked beneath. The crown prince appeared at the door as the light from the torches danced on the walls. He removed his cloak and approached me in a sheer loincloth, his eyes gleaming. He motioned to me to stand on the bed and held my legs to his chest.

"You are the sun of my life," he whispered. My soul delighted in his presence, but my body cringed. He continued, "I fell in love with you at the Sed festival. That night I hurried to my mother and told her I wanted to make you my wife." He laughed joyfully. "At first she denied me my request. She did not want me to marry a girl with no royal blood. When I reminded her that neither was she of royal blood, she feigned anger and dismissed the subject. The next thing she told me was that she had met with you—and she gave me her approval."

I recalled how Tiye had claimed that my marriage to the crown prince was her idea. I hid my smile. I felt as though I was expected to speak. I wanted what I said to be the truth.

"I believed in your God before I even saw you."

"What joy!" he cried. "You heard from Ay?"

I nodded. "You are the first woman to believe, Nefertiti," he said.

I wanted to speak to him longer, to delay the moment when we would lie together. "I want to be the first to sing hymns in his temple."

"I promise you that," he whispered, and kissed me. "You shall bear me an heir to the throne." Suddenly, all the magnificent emotions I had felt disappeared. All that remained was reticence and irritation.

We continued to walk our path together, both as man and wife and as believers. I delved further into the faith with him. His spirit engulfed me and filled me with so much light that I expected God might speak to me as he had spoken to him. As for my body, it convulsed silently every time he came near me. His seed grew inside me. I became pale and ill, as the child within me made a mockery of my beautiful, slender body. Akhenaten dwelled in the truth. He despised all lies and falsehood. I wondered how I would reply if he ever asked me, "Do you love me, Nefertiti?" I knew I could not find the courage to lie to him. I tried to be prepared. "Love will come in time," I would tell him. I would ask his forgiveness and explain to him that he had taught me to love the truth. Perhaps it would have brought an end to my dreams even before I became queen. But he never asked.

One day Queen Tiye called for me, and as I approached her she looked at me closely. "You must mind your health," she started. "You are carrying a precious life within you that will soon be part of the history of this country."

"Pray for me, my Queen."

"You have a long life ahead of you," she said confidently. "Do not let fear control your mind."

"Some things are not in the hands of people," I replied.

"A queen is more than just 'people.'" She heaved a sigh.

The queen was destroying my defenses. What a powerful woman she was, just as my father had always described her. My husband loved her dearly, and she regarded him as her sole property. Even after our marriage, I felt the weight of her shackles.

The news about the One God reached the priests and the strife began. During that time I had grown to know the extent of the power my husband possessed within his feeble body. I felt the strength of his spirit, and the intensity of his courage and determination.

"All the stones of the pyramids cannot move me from my position," he said to me once.

"And I am with you," I replied.

"Our God shall not forsake us," he cried.

Even his mother could not persuade him to change his stand. One day, Tiye called me to her chamber. When I walked in I realized that this was perhaps the most important day in my life.

"Has the pregnancy distracted you from following the affairs of Thebes?" she asked.

"The affairs of Thebes are my affairs." I was prepared for a battle.

"Did your kind words have no influence on your husband?" she asked.

"The words of his God are more powerful."

"You do not seem saddened or worried."

"I believe in what he says, my Queen." My wrists were free at last. With that declaration, I made it known that my love for my God was stronger than my love for the throne.

Tiye glared. "Do you really believe in the Sole Creator?"

"Yes, my Queen."

"You renounce the deities of Egypt?"

"God is one and has no partner," I replied.

"Do you believe that other people have the right to worship their gods?"

"My God is not a threat to anyone."

"But one day your husband will be king, and he must serve all the deities."

"We serve no other but the One and Only."

"Your rebellion," she cried, "shall have the gravest repercussions."

"God will never forsake us."

"You promised me your unconditional loyalty," she said bitterly.

"You are my queen. But God is above all else."

I returned to my quarters with a heavy heart and tearful eyes. I did not know what destiny held in store for me. Yet I felt at peace. Soon the prince was ordered to tour the empire. I felt that Tiye had begun her punishment. She meant to deprive me of my husband when I was going to deliver my child at any moment. When Akhenaten left, I was gripped by new emotions. The light of life had gone; even the sun had only darkness. I was choked with fear. Nothing could compensate for my husband's absence, not even having my stepmother, Tey, by my side. I was enshrouded in sorrow. I missed Akhenaten wherever I was and at every hour of the day. I could not believe that he had occupied so much of my life. I realized that, without him, I was not happy. It was then that I became aware that I loved him, not only as my spiritual companion, but as husband and lover. Bitter tears seared my face. I regretted my ignorance and my blindness. I longed for him to return so that I could throw myself at his feet.

Queen Tiye and I went into labor at the same time. I had Meretaten, and the queen bore twins, Smenkhkare and Tutankhamun. When I found out that I had given birth to a girl I was overcome with grief. I heard the whispers of the harem saying that it was the curse of the priests of Amun. They said I would never bear a son as long as I lived.

Around that time, King Amenhotep III married Tadukhipa, the daughter of Tushratta, king of Mitanni, to reinforce the ties of friendship between Egypt and Mitanni. Tadukhipa's beauty was renowned. She entered Thebes in a magnificient procession with three hundred slaves. Tey tried to entertain me by talking about the new princess in the palace. She spoke to me of her wealth and beauty, but added at the end that, of course, no sun shone more brightly than mine. King Amenhotep III adored Tadukhipa, his new bride who was the age of his grandchildren. But the king was not able to savor his newfound happiness for long. For word arrived that the crown prince was preaching his religion throughout the provinces. I was summoned to appear before the king and queen. I did not expect to see the king so frail, but it seemed that he had exhausted himself in the pleasures of life.

"He is mad," the king cried viciously.

"We can send the armed forces to the provinces to correct the damage that has been done," Tiye said.

"He has lost the succession to the throne. Nothing we do will help him regain it."

"Perhaps he will succeed. Perhaps they will heed his words," I said after a moment's hesitation.

"You are foolish, Nefertiti," the king shouted. "Just like your husband."

"You could have tried to make him more reasonable," Tiye added. "Instead you joined him in his nonsense."

"How can I achieve what you have failed to do, my Queen?" I replied, trying to control my anger.

"You deliberately encourage him," she said accusingly.

"When he returns," Amenhotep interrupted with a wave of his hand, "I will have him choose between the throne and his religion."

My sadness grew. The morning after I met with the king and queen, Tiye woke me up and whispered, "The king is dead, Queen Nefertiti."

My heart was heavy with grief. I wondered if before

he died King Amenhotep III had carried out his threat. Would Tiye sacrifice her beloved son? One time, when she was overseeing the mummification of her husband, she called me and said, "I want you to know that the priests requested that I appoint Smenkhkare or Tutankhamun king and that I should be regent."

I feared what Tiye would say next. "Your decision shall be the wisest, and I will embrace it regardless," I replied.

"Are you speaking the truth?" she asked.

"What else do I have but the truth?" I replied desperately.

"I denied them their request. My love for my son was greater than my wisdom."

I felt as though I had just begun to breathe. I was speechless.

"Are you happy?"

"Yes, my Queen," I replied earnestly. "I abhor lying."

"Do you promise me to defend the traditions?"

"I cannot promise that."

"You deserve to be punished," she said. "But I also admire you. You and Akhenaten have chosen your path, so walk it. It is what the gods charted."

I returned to my quarters elated. I showered Meretaten with kisses. Then my beloved returned from his journey. I hurried to him and threw my arms around him.

"At last your love has come, Nefertiti," he said calmly.

I was startled and said, "I loved you even before I laid eyes on you."

"But only now, you love me as your husband." I was stunned by his ability to discern the secrets of the heart.

After the burial of Amenhotep III, Akhenaten came to me with tearful eyes. "Death frightens me," he said. "I did not love my father as I should have." We ascended the throne surrounded by hostility and apprehension. Akhenaten called upon his men to join his religion. They declared their faith willingly. It never occurred to me to doubt their faith, until much later when they all abandoned him to save themselves. Except for Meri-Ra, the high priest of the One God. I believe that Akhenaten knew that they were not sincere. But he believed that love was the cure for all ills. He thought that in time their faith would grow deeper with love, and that they would believe in him. He waited patiently for their faith, as he had once waited for my love. But they were not deserving. Some of them even harbored a secret desire to claim the throne after him—Haremhab, and even my father, Ay. Do not think that my bitterness has led me to fabricate this. I do not rely on mere impressions either. I learned these facts from conversations I had with the men during the last days of Akhetaten. I was pleased that the priests decided to entrust the throne to Tutankhamun instead. I believe the others still dwell on their old dream.

Despite the hostility that surrounded us when we first took the throne, Akhenaten and I were extremely happy. Meretaten was beginning to crawl, and a new life was growing inside me. Akhenaten had no other partner but me. He inherited his father's harem, with the beautiful Mitannian woman, but he abstained from visiting it. Then Queen Tiye came and I expected no good from her visit.

"Akhenaten," she started, close enough that I could hear her, "you are king now. You must not neglect your harem."

"I have but one love, just as I have one God," he laughed.

"But you must be fair. Do not forget that Tadukhipa is in your harem. She deserves to be treated well, if only for her father Tushratta's sake." Tiye glanced at me and noticed my irritation. She continued, "Nefertiti has proven to be a wise queen. Perhaps she will agree with me about your harem."

I remained silent, trying not to reveal that I was upset. Tiye continued to talk about the duties of a queen.

I became curious about the harem, particularly Tadukhipa. I visited them, saying merely that I wanted to make their acquaintance. Tadukhipa was indeed beautiful, but my self-confidence was not shaken. We exchanged a few words, and parted enemies.

The next day, as I sat with my husband in the palace garden, I found myself asking him, "What do you intend to do about the harem?"

"I do not want it," he replied simply.

"But the queen mother does not heed your desires," I complained.

"My mother loves tradition."

"But you do not believe in tradition."

"You're quite right, my beloved," he laughed.

I suppose it was around that time that I met with the high priest of Amun.

"My Queen," the high priest started, "perhaps you know what I have come for."

"I am listening, High Priest," I replied without enthusiasm.

"Let the king worship whichever god he pleases. But all the deities, Amun in particular, have the right to be worshiped," he pleaded.

"We are not trying to harm your god."

"I am hoping that when the time comes you will support us."

"I can only promise what I know I can give."

"Your father and I are old friends. And I know that nothing can spoil our friendship."

"I am glad to hear that."

When he left I knew I had made an eternal enemy. Akhenaten devoted his time to the religion. He called for love, abolished punishment, and relieved the poor of their dues. People began to believe that it was a new era of love and benevolence. I gave birth to my second daughter, Meketaten. Once more I was disappointed and remembered all that had been said about the curse of the priests. But Akhenaten loved his daughters. "The crown prince will come when it is his time," he said to comfort me. We built a temple for the One God in Thebes and went to visit it for the first time. The priests had gathered a mob of their followers and they stood outside the temple calling the name of Amun. The king was dismayed. He spent the night on the terrace of our room, addressing Thebes: "O city of evil, home of the lustful god, and merciless priests, O Thebes, I will never dwell in you." The voice of God told him to build a new city. Bek the sculptor selected eighty thousand men and started work on the city of the Sole Creator. Meanwhile, we continued to live in Thebes, happy inside our palace, yet surrounded on all sides by malice. I bore two more girls, Ankhesenpaaten and Nefernaten. Then we moved to the new city. Smenkhkare and Tutankhamun came with us, but Tiye decided to remain in Thebes to preserve the last tie between the throne and the priests of Amun.

When we reached Akhetaten, the city of light, I cried with bliss, "How great is your beauty, how sweet is your spirit, O God of this city and of the universe." We prayed in the temple, and sang the hymns of the One God. Meri-Ra was appointed high priest of the Sole Creator. We lived in pure happiness, until one day the king returned from his solitude with a solemn look.

"My God commands me that no other deity should be worshiped in his country."

I realized instantly the gravity of what he said. "And what will become of the other deities?"

"I will decree the closing of their temples and appropriate their endowments." He was determined. I remained silent. "You do not seem happy, Nefertiti."

"You are defying the priests of the entire land," I replied.

"Yes. It is in my power."

"If you do so, you are bound to use violence and punishment. You are a man of peace. Why resort to such measures?"

"I shall never use violence as long as I live."

"What if they disobey you?"

"I will distribute the endowments of the temples to the poor of the country and call upon them to worship the One God and abandon the other deities."

I felt at once as though a weight had been lifted from my chest. I kissed him. "God will never forsake you."

The decree was made and executed without provoking the storms I had expected. It was God's power, and the power of the throne. We became more confident. In the evenings we visited the different quarters of Akhetaten in our royal carriage. The people received us with adulation. We descended from our carriage and walked among them under the palm trees, defying the long tradition that separated the royalty and the common people. We became so familiar with them that we knew their names and faces and professions. Love replaced the old fear in the people's hearts. The hymns of the One and Only were heard all over Akhetaten.

"I am afraid you are diminishing the traditional status of the king," my father told me once.

"Father," I replied laughing, "we only dwell in the truth."

Then we went on our journey through the empire, calling the people to worship the Sole Creator. Our enemies were in awe of our success. Maho, the chief of police, told us about the priests' attempts to win the people over to their side by slandering the king and the throne. But we took little notice. People grew accustomed to Akhenaten's peculiar ways of worship, his solitariness, and his complete devotion. I suppose it was I who became a mystery in their eyes. How could I be so immersed in worship, when I had to manage all the administrative and financial affairs of the country? Perhaps they even questioned the sincerity of my faith. The truth is that I believed every word Akhenaten uttered. I shared his faith and his life. "When all the spirits have become pure and free of any evil," he used to say, "everyone will hear the voice of God and we shall all dwell in the truth." That was his real purpose, that everyone should dwell in the truth. When we returned from our journey we found Meketaten sick and bedridden. Her face was so pale that we hardly recognized the daughter we had created. Akhenaten remained by her side, praying. I asked Bento, the physician, to save her.

"Bento," I said, calling him to the corner of Meketaten's room, "my daughter is dying."

"I did all that I could," he said mournfully.

"The priests have cast a spell to deprive Akhenaten of his most beloved daughter," I cried in horror.

"Do not burn my heart with the grief of mourning her, dear God," I heard Akhenaten whisper. "I love her and cannot live without her in my life. She is far wiser than her age, O God. If you spare her life she will spend it in your service."

But Meketaten's soul faded until she left our world and ascended to the stars in God's Kingdom. We threw ourselves upon her, wailing, abandoned to grief.

"Why, O God?" Akhenaten cried. "Why do you try my faith so very severely? Must you be so cruel in showing me that I still do not know your mighty power? Why do you treat me so harshly when you are full of compassion, so coldly when you are love, so angrily when I am your obedient servant? Why do you insist on being a mystery when you are the light? Why did you make her so beautiful, and give her such sound reason? Why did you make us love her, and prepare her for your service? O Mighty God, why?"

We remained in mourning until the sorrows of the country pulled us out of our grief to face a tragedy. We conferred with Nakht and he told us the details of the strife and the rebellion that had swept the empire. I must admit that my determination was no longer as firm as it had been before Meketaten died. But Akhenaten endured the most severe storms, as if he were the Great Pyramid, imperishable.

"God will persevere," he said. "I will not compromise."

I was encouraged by his strength of spirit, and my strength returned afresh. My misgivings subsided, and I felt remorse for my momentary weakness. Then the queen mother, Tiye, visited us in Akhetaten. First she met with our men in her palace in southern Akhetaten. Then she summoned me and my husband.

"The skies are filled with dark clouds," she began. "Your men have given me their word of honor that they will remain loyal to you under any circumstances."

"Do you trust them?" I asked curiously.

"In times like this, I am compelled to lend them my trust," she replied reproachfully.

"My God will be victorious," Akhenaten said.

"Soon the country will be consumed by civil wars." She was incensed.

"God will never forsake me," he repeated.

"I cannot speak for the gods, but I can speak for what transpires in the world of people."

"Mother," he said sadly, "you do not believe."

"Do not speak to me of the unknown. Speak to me as the king that you are and heed me as a queen. You must act before it is too late. Use the armed forces to protect your borders from the enemies. Use the guards and the police to stop the corruption inside the empire. Hurry, before your throne is lost to the enemies."

"I shall not have one drop of blood shed."

"Do not make me regret that I entrusted you with the throne."

"I only believe in the throne as a means to serve God."

Tiye looked at me and said, "Speak, Nefertiti—perhaps the gods meant you to marry him so that you can save him this very moment."

"Our God will not forsake us, Mother," I replied.

"Madness has won." She was desperate.

Tiye left the palace sad and ill. She returned to Thebes, where she lived only a few days more, then died with her worries. A few days later, Haremhab, Nakht, and my father Ay asked to speak with us.

"Your faces betray bad news," Akhenaten said.

"We have come because of our love for Egypt and the empire," my father began.

"What about your faith in the Sole Creator?"

"We still believe in him. But we are responsible for our lives, too, not only our faith."

"This responsibility you speak of is worthless if it is not inspired by faith," Akhenaten added.

"The enemies of the empire have crossed our borders," Nakht said. "The provinces are in open rebellion. We are trapped in Akhetaten."

"God will not forsake me, and I will not forsake his teachings," he insisted.

"We are facing a civil war!" Haremhab said.

"There shall be no wars."

"Are we to wait until we are slain like sheep?" Haremhab asked.

"I myself will confront the army that attacks us, alone and unarmed," the king said.

"They will kill you and then come after us. If you insist on upholding your message, then relinquish the throne and devote yourself to religion."

"I will not forsake the throne of my God. It would be treachery. I release you from your vow of loyalty to me."

"We will leave you some time to decide," Haremhab said.

They delivered their last warning and left us. I never imagined a pharaoh could be so humiliated. I wondered why God was so harsh on us, but Akhenaten's faith was not shaken. I admired his determination.

Then Haremhab asked to meet me privately. "Act now," he said. "Do whatever is in your power. If he insists on his position, he will be killed. He may be slain by his own men! You must act promptly."

I was bewildered. I saw the ghastly shadows of death and defeat. My faith was shaken. I felt the torment of helplessness. How could I save my beloved? It occurred to me that if I left him he might falter and take the advice of his men. He would be convinced that I had betrayed him, but at least his life would be saved. Thus I left my beloved king and husband, my heart seared with grief. I went to the palace in northern Akhetaten. My sister, Mutnedjmet, visited me and told me that the king had not wavered from his position. She told me that the men had decided that in order to save him, they must abandon him and pledge their allegiance to the new pharaoh, Tutankhamun.

"When will you move to Thebes?" she asked.

"A part of the old prophecy has come true," I said, reading the meaning between her words. "Now it is time for the other part. So you go to Thebes in peace, Mutnedjmet. I will stay here beside my husband and my God."

Sadness set its roots deep in my heart, as though I had never once been happy in my life. I was haunted by guilt as I watched from my window the people leaving the city of light before the curse claimed them. I heard their voices, the cries of their children, and the howling of their dogs. I saw them come in waves, carrying whatever they could salvage of happier days. They hurried toward the Nile, the north, and the south. I watched until I saw the last of them leave the city. Akhetaten was deserted. Gloom hung over the magnificent houses, the gardens, and the streets. "Akhetaten," I cried, "O city of light, where are the hymns and melodies, where is the victory, where is love? Where are you, my God? Why did you forsake us?"

The city was now empty except for two prisoners—my beloved and I—and a few guards appointed by the priests. When I wished to return to his palace to see him and talk with him, the guards stopped me. I was not allowed to leave the palace, they said. They did not allow me even to write to him. I knew then that there was nothing I could do but await my death in this prison. I tried sending messages to the new pharaoh and to my father and Haremhab, stating my simple request to see Akhenaten. But the guards told me I was allowed no contact with the outside world. I waited patiently and without hope for my days to end. I was no longer aware of the passage of time. I prayed constantly, until I finally regained all my faith in the One God. Indeed, I believe now that the final victory will be for the Sole Creator.

The chief of the guards came to me one day and said, "I am ordered to tell you that the heretic has died after a long illness. A royal party has been sent to mummify and entomb him according to the royal rituals."

I did not believe a word he said. My beloved did not fall ill and die. They must have killed him. His soul now rests eternally. One day I shall follow him. I will explain to him why I left him and ask his forgiveness, and he will seat me beside him on the throne of truth.

————

Queen Nefertiti was quiet, her sweet voice stilled. I bade her farewell, dreading the path that took me away from her. My heart was infused with her beauty.

When I returned to Sais, my father greeted me happily. He asked me about my journey, and I answered him. For days we talked and I recounted the details of my travels. I told my father everything I had learned, except for two things—my growing fondness for the hymns of the One God, and my profound love for the beautiful Nefertiti.